WITHOUT WARNING

WITHOUT WARNING

Anthony G. Shea Jr.
Major, USAF Retired

WORD ASSOCIATION PUBLISHERS
www.wordassociation.com
1.800.827.7903

www.anthonyshea.com

Edited by Ted Gilley
Edit\ Understudied by Megan Shea.
Cover design inspired by John C. Shea.

Copyright © 2011 by Anthony G. Shea, Jr.

All rights reserved. No part of this book may be used or reproduced in any manner whatsoever without written permission of the author.

Printed in the United States of America.

ISBN: 978-1-59571-671-2

Library of Congress Control Number: 2011928118

Designed and published by

Word Association Publishers
205 Fifth Avenue
Tarentum, Pennsylvania 15084

www.wordassociation.com
1.800.827.7903

This book is dedicated to
my loving wife, Kerry.

TABLE OF CONTENTS

ABOUT THE AUTHOR
Anthony G. Shea 9
CHAPTER 1
Reflections. 11
CHAPTER 2
The Last Normal Day,
Wednesday, February 8, 2012 17
CHAPTER 3
Hectic Day at White House. 22
CHAPTER 4
Route 28 Blues 24
CHAPTER 5
The Graveyard Shift. 26
CHAPTER 6
Chaos. 31
CHAPTER 7
Safety 34
CHAPTER 8
Impact 44
CHAPTER 9
A Bad Day for the Earth 51
CHAPTER 10
The Cool Down. 59
CHAPTER 11
Day 3: Room Temperature 63
CHAPTER 12
Day 4: Getting Cooler. 70
CHAPTER 13
Day 5: Below Freezing. 76
CHAPTER 14
Day 6: The Coming Storm 81
CHAPTER 15
1 Week: Normalcy. 85
CHAPTER 16
The Blizzard 89
CHAPTER 17
Refuge 92
CHAPTER 18
Contact: Week 4 96
CHAPTER 19
Maternity. 99
CHAPTER 20
Light!. 105

CHAPTER 21
The Warming 111
CHAPTER 22
The Journey Home 116
CHAPTER 23
Census 121
CHAPTER 24
Anomaly 124
CHAPTER 25
Refined Pictures 128
CHAPTER 26
Extraction 131
CHAPTER 27
Reverse Engineering 137
CHAPTER 28
Moving Day. 140
CHAPTER 29
Below the Surface 143
CHAPTER 30
December 21, 2013:
Another Asteroid. 147
CHAPTER 31
Spring 2014 151
CHAPTER 32
Coming Out of Hibernation 154
CHAPTER 33
Invasion: August 27, 2014 160
CHAPTER 34
Abduction 166
CHAPTER 35
Lay of the Land 173
CHAPTER 36
Homeward Bound. 176
CHAPTER 37
The Jig is Up. 179
CHAPTER 38
By a Hair 185
CHAPTER 39
The Plan. 190
CHAPTER 40
Plan Execution 195
CHAPTER 41
The Battle 203
CHAPTER 42
Terms of Surrender 206
CHAPTER 43
War Crimes 210
CHAPTER 44
Coexistence 213

ABOUT THE AUTHOR
Anthony G. Shea

Anthony G. Shea Jr. hails from Leechburg, Pennsylvania. He is a 1985 graduate of Leechburg High School and enlisted in the U.S. Air Force the same year. Anthony served three enlisted tours of duty as a security policeman (1985-1994); these assignments were at Myrtle Beach Air Force Base, South Carolina; Suwon Air Base, Republic of Korea; and Patrick Air Force Base, Florida. In law enforcement, Anthony worked as a gate sentry, patrolman, aircraft security, prison guard, 911 dispatcher, and head of vehicle registration and identification. While enlisted, Anthony earned his Associates of Science degree in Criminal Justice (1989) from the Community College of the Air Force, and then a Bachelor of Science in Computer Studies (1993) from the University of Maryland. While serving in the Air Force, and attending to night classes, Anthony also worked a second job as a Dominos Pizza deliveryman to offset tuition costs. After graduation, Anthony applied to and was accepted for Officers Training School and commissioned a second lieutenant as a communications officer. Prior to commissioning, Anthony had worked his way up to staff sergeant in the enlisted ranks. Anthony served three tours of duty in communications. His assignments were at Air Force Global Weather Central, Offutt Air Force Base, Nebraska; Air Force Space Command, Peterson Air Force Base, Colorado; and the Defense Information Systems Agency-Europe, Stuttgart, Germany. Anthony worked in various facets of communications ranging from Unix Systems administration to Wide Area Networks supporting meteorological and space assets such as the Defense Meteorological Satellite Program, Global Positioning System, and Ground-based Electro Optical Deep Space Surveillance system. Anthony also worked on the European military internet and voice systems; during this time, he earned a Master of Arts Degree in Telecommunications Management from Webster University (1998). Anthony broadened his career in the Air Force, taking a position as an assistant professor of military doctrine and history at the Virginia Military Institute in Lexington, Virginia. Anthony also oversaw recruiting support for a four-state area, based out of Canonsburg, Pennsylvania. Anthony retired from the Air Force in 2008 with the rank of major and is currently employed with the Bank of New York Mellon as a business relations liaison. Anthony currently serves as the Elks West Central District Chairman for Drug Awareness and Lodge Hoop Shoot Chairman. He is married Kerry; they have four children, Anthony III, Megan, Ellie, and Abigail.

CHAPTER 1
Reflections

"Imaginary evils soon become real ones by indulging our reflections on them."
JOHN RUSKIN

My name is Regis Steele. I have been wheelchair-bound my entire life. Even with the hand I've been dealt, I have made a good life for myself. I am married, with a child on the way, and I made a very good living as a technical writer. I have lived as full a life as could be expected, and one better than most, even with my handicap. Some say that on the phone I sound just like the actor John Wayne; people always say I sound so big and burly on the phone. When people finally meet me in person, they always have the same shocked look when they see that I am only four-foot-eight and a buck ten. I also let them off the hook easy when they first realize that I am handicapped.

When I was growing up, my dad, Robert Steele, tried to do everything he could to make my life seem as normal as possible. He was a man's man who could praise me, or anyone, and make me—or whoever it was he was talking to—feel either on top of the world, only to feel his wrath and disappointment if you strayed from his core values. He carried these traits over from his days at the Virginia Military Institute, and ten years of active duty in the army after that. We moved a lot in his army days. Dad later became a corporate executive known for his no-nonsense approach in dealing effectively with just about everything he encountered; he could think himself out of about any fix that was thrown his way. I looked up to my dad all my life.

We settled down in Dad's childhood home just outside the sleepy western Pennsylvania town of Leechburg, on the land he inherited from his dad, after he got out of the army in 1980. Dad stayed in the Pennsylvania Army National Guard for the next twenty-five years, even serving his last Guard tour as an assistant to the Pennsylvania adjutant general. My dad retired as a bird colonel. Once Dad made the rank of colonel, that is what I and everyone else called him from that point on—the Colonel.

The Colonel lived on the property he inherited, or at least what was left from the tract that originally came from my dad's great-great-great-great- grandfather, who earned it for fighting in the Revolutionary War. My ancestor received a land patent just after the United States had become a country. A lot of blood, sweat, and tears had gone into this land by the Steele family over the generations and various generations were buried on the same land.

The Colonel told me the most amazing story when I was a young boy about "the cave." At the time, we lived thousands of miles away at an army base in Hawaii. At first, I did not even believe him. I thought of his stories of "the cave" sounded pretty crazy.

He talked of a cave that was as big as a basketball court inside, with an underground river deep in one of the tunnels on Pap's land. The Colonel said this same underground river had gained fame further downstream at the turn of the last century with the whiskey distillery just over the hill from the Colonel's house. But what intrigued me the most about the Colonel's story was of the many Indian drawings he said there were on the cavern walls. The Colonel said he couldn't even adequately explain them to me but that I'd have to wait see them for myself someday when we were back in CONUS—that is military speak for the Continental United States.

I was ten years old on the day in 1977 that the Red Cross came to our door at base housing at Scholfield barracks in Hawaii. A nicely dressed army man, another man in a suit and tie, and a priest came for my dad, Captain Robert Steele. My mom knew sort of knew why these three men were there, but I was still very naive at that point in my life. Dad was still at his job at the base headquarters building when they finally caught up with him. They told my dad that his dad, my grandfather, Pap, had died.

I vividly remember the flight home the next evening. It was on a contract Boeing 747 aircraft used by the Department of Defense for moving troops between the Pacific assignments and St. Louis, Missouri. The Colonel was nicely dressed in his army uniform for the flight back to Leechburg, Pennsylvania.

What I remember most was Dad letting me have the window seat on the long flight over the Pacific Ocean. I was amazed, looking out over the vast body of water below and up at the stars above. The almost full moon reflected off the water below. Later we flew over a thunderstorm, and the lightning lit up the clouds; the plane bounced in the turbulence. The plane's engine hummed its continuous din and I faded in and out of sleep.

We attended Pap's funeral two days later. It was the first time in my life that I ever saw my father cry. Not many people came to Pap's funeral. My grandfather had been kind of a loner. A lot of folks whispered over the years, saying Pap was a little eccentric, especially after Grandma passed nine years earlier of cancer. My dad was Pap's only child. Not for lack of trying, but my grandma gave up trying to have more children after several miscarriages in a row after my dad was born.

About five years before his death, Pap had received a large cash settlement from a class action lawsuit resulting from

Grandma working the nuclear plant in Parks Township near Vandergrift. A steel worker by trade at Allegheny Ludlum in Natrona, Pap did alright in life, making a living. And of course, Pap owned 128 acres of land overlooking the Allegheny River—a lot of it useless hillside—with about twenty or so acres on top, with a pond and an old stone farm house.

While we were home on emergency leave for my pap's funeral, the Colonel finally took me to the cave. The Colonel had to carry me down over the hill on his back from Pap's house. Pap had built a trail down over a hill since the last time the Colonel had been home, but it was not wheelchair accessible. The cave entrance had a steel door over it and was locked.

"This is new," the Colonel said, eyeing the solid-looking door over the entrance. "By the looks of the door, you would need a tank to open it," he exclaimed, pulling on the handle.

"Wait a moment, I'll be right back, Rege," he said, having one of those eureka moments.

It had just hit dad just then, the supervisor at Clawson's Funeral Home in Leechburg had given him a single key that he had found around Pap's neck on a chain with his dog tags.

The Colonel left me by myself at the cave entrance and went back up to the house to get the key. As I sat there alone on the rocks, I noticed the blackened rock overhang above the enclosed door over the cave entrance. I did not know it then, but the blackened overhang was from the fires that must have burned inside the cave over the eons by the Native Americans. On the rock face below the overlook, I could have sworn I saw several hieroglyphs. Just then, the Colonel came back down with the key.

"Yep, this is what it was for," he said as he put the key in the keyhole.

When I first looked in the cavern, I could not see anything until my eyes adjusted to the darkness. An immense cool breeze hit us, as we entered through the door; the whole place had sort of a musty, dingy smell to it, water dripping echoed in the distance. Just then, the Colonel hit a switch at the entrance and several large lights running off car batteries turned on from the roof of the cavern; they weren't overly bright, but the entire cavern became visible.

"Guess we won't need the flashlights," the Colonel said, looking up in amazement.

"The cave is huge," was all I could exclaim!

I could hear my voice echo as I said "Wow." I then said, "Echo" and heard my voice again.

Pap had built a cabin within the cave, totally dwarfed by the enormity of the cavern itself. I could now hear flowing water in the distance from what I guessed was the underground river the Colonel had talked about in his tales.

Pap was weird at best; he had stockpiled all kinds of supplies in the cabin in the cave from food to clothes to guns. One room in had all kinds of radio equipment and maps. Pap also had decorated all the walls with Pittsburgh Steelers memorabilia; he even had a signed photograph of Terry Bradshaw.

The Colonel said, "Pap must have been busy over the last few years of his life while we were all away overseas," as he looked around the cabin.

The Colonel was in awe of Pap's efforts. "We now know where his cash settlement must have went," he said.

We took it as a bomb shelter, being at almost at the height of the Cold War at the time. I still remember how tensions were high between the United States and the Soviet Union; I used to have nightmares about nuclear wars when I was a kid. I wonder now if what Pap did was for something else, and was Pap really all that crazy?.

As amazing as this cabin in the cave was, the Colonel finally showed me the Indian cave paintings we had talked about from the time I had memory of anything as a young child. The paintings were of animals, people, and villages; they looked normal, if you could call them that. But there was this one set of drawings that seemed totally out of the ordinary, if any of this could seem real or ordinary. It showed an Indian village along a river, with a large triangle over it. The triangle had what looked like flames coming down from it, and below the triangle it showed everyone sleeping. This image has been burnt into my mind as the most vivid childhood memory I had. The Colonel made me swear I'd never tell anyone about the cave because like his father he believed that the government would take the land from his family in the name of some natural history or eminent domain land grab.

We stayed in Leechburg for about a week while the Colonel took care of Pap's unfinished business regarding his estate. We stayed in Pap's house during this time. I enjoyed looking at all his books and magazines. Pap must have had fifteen different subscriptions to various hunting, medical, country living, firearms, and survival type publications. In the will, the Colonel (and I, unknowing at the time) had inherited a considerable sum of money, stocks, coins, and of course the land and house. But the Colonel was in the army, so we had to go back to Hawaii—duty called.

The Colonel locked the entrance to the cave before we left; he then stacked some brush over the door to conceal the cave entrance the best he could. The Colonel hired a caretaker to watch over the house, cut the grass, and get the mail. My mom, dad, and I got back on the airplane at the Pittsburgh airport for the TWA flight to St. Louis, and then the contract 747 flight to Hawaii. As on the way to St. Louis, the contract flight had numerous stops along the way at military bases with soldiers, sailors, and airman getting on and off the airplane. In a few weeks, we were back to our old lives at Scholfield Barracks in Hawaii. But I never forgot my visit to the cave.

CHAPTER 2
The Last Normal Day, Wednesday, February 8, 2012

> *"Normal day, let me be aware of the treasure you are... Let me not pass you by in quest of some rare and perfect Tomorrow. One day I shall dig my nails into the earth, or bury my face in my pillow, or stretch myself taut, or raise my hands to the sky and want, more than all the world, your return."*
>
> Mary Jean Iron

They say there are certain events in your life after which you will remember exactly where you were, and what you were doing, when that something happened. I was not alive at the time when President John F. Kennedy was assassinated. I do, however, remember exactly where I was when the space shuttle Challenger exploded in 1986. I was in my college dorm at Penn State, eating pizza for breakfast in the day room. For 9/11, I was driving, with my then future wife, Kaitlin along I-68 near Frostburg, Maryland, to talk to a future employer about working on a technical manual for a new Kodak digital camera. And of course, I remember back to the day when I found out Pap had died. I remember the army staff car and the men who came to the door. I also remember seeing the cave for the first time.

I woke up in the middle of the night that day with insomnia. Though it was not an everyday occurrence, I enjoyed listening to my iPod Nano radio on those sleepless nights. I listened to my favorite radio show, *Coast to Coast with George Noory*. It is one of those programs you had to take with a grain of salt, but fascinating just the same. Some of the shows I recall over the years were about global warming, various government cover-ups, Bigfoot, UFOs, and other supernatural occurrences.

That early morning, as I lay there, I listened as some doctor told George Noory about how the government had infected people with the flu from diamond-shaped aircraft around the world. From the news reports on regular TV so far, this flu didn't appear any more dangerous than the swine flu scare of 2009. But, the doctor on the late-night talk show claimed a lot of folks in the Third World were dying daily and that it was a government cover-up.

The doctor told Noory, "The western world got this strain of flu mainly under control with vaccines and antibiotics."

It was true there was a flu pandemic, by the definition of the Centers for Disease Control. Primarily, the pandemic was rampant in less-developed parts of the world such as South America and Africa. There, the people suffered from it much more because of the lack of modern medicine and antibiotics.

The doctor said the origin of this new flu strain was unknown and was a conspiracy by the "global government" to reduce the population in the Third World nations and assume control of their lands for their natural resources; the doctor also said the casualties from the bug were grossly under-reported by the media.

About normal for a George Noory radio show, I thought as I listened to the commercials about hybrid seeds and buying gold bullion. I always listened with my head set on, so as not to wake up Kaitlin.

The weather was horrible outside that morning, with over a foot of snow on the ground and a temperature just above zero. This day would be a day I'd dial in and work from home. My boss wouldn't care as long as I got the work done. I liked it, too, because I would not get a thousand interruptions, like I would in the office. Kaitlin was already starting to get ready for her job at the ABC Academy Day Care, just about a mile out of town.

Kaitlin was usually out the door by 4:45 a.m. to get to her job by 5:00 to open up for the parents commuting to work in Pittsburgh. I lived on the same road as the Colonel and Mom; the Colonel had broken off a piece of land for Kaitlin and me as a wedding gift ten years ago.

They say there is someone for everyone, and my love was Kaitlin. Kaitlin and I had met during our freshman year in college. My handicap did not concern her, and Mom and Dad loved her as if she were their own child.

The house Kaitlin and I built was modest but comfortable. We had it equipped with the needed modifications for my handicap. With Kaitlin being four months pregnant, and my job going exceptionally well, life was about as good as it gets.

After years of us trying, Kaitlin had finally gotten pregnant with the help of fertility treatments. Not a moment too soon: she was forty and I was forty-three, and both of our biological clocks were ticking.

I had a lot of optimism that day, even with my insomnia and the cold and snowy weather outside.

Kaitlin gave me a kiss on the cheek that morning and said, "I love you," as she did every morning; she then headed off to work.

I remember the smell of her perfume, and the outfit she wore and the sweet pout of her lower lip. I remember the distinct sound the garage door made as it opened and then closed as Kaitlin drove off in her new Kia Borrego. I made a mental note to ask the Colonel to oil the rails of the garage door with WD-40 soon. I even remember the exact cereal I ate that morning, and the color of the bowl.

By 7 a.m., my brother in law John, or Johnnie as we all called him, was already on his way to Pittsburgh for his job at Highmark Insurance in the U.S. Steel building. Though only related to me through the marriage of my wife's sister, we got along pretty well. The Colonel liked him too—for his being in the military for four years. Johnnie worked as manager of some sort; but he still had the disposition of a professional soldier from his service in the army. His wife, Missy, Kaitlin's younger sister, had just found out she was also pregnant. I swear they must have timed this out. They lived only a couple miles away on the main road going into town. Missy worked at the Armstrong County Memorial Hospital in Kittanning as a registered nurse. On that day, she called off due to the weather.

The Colonel called me about 8 a.m. that morning and asked if I could come over for about half an hour; his truck's battery was completely dead from the cold and he needed a ride to town to buy a new battery. What surprised me about the Colonel was that he was extremely successful, a true secret millionaire, and lived the most modest lifestyle. He had one truck, a 1957 Chevrolet in immaculate condition, he lived in the same farm house his father, grandfather, and great-grandfather had lived in, and had lived in my childhood home ever since he got out of the military.

As important as he became in life, he was the most humble, down-to-earth man I ever knew, and that's not being biased because he was my dad. The Colonel treated everyone like they were the most important person in the world.

I told the Colonel I'd come over in a few minutes and we'd drive to Bob Myers's alternator and battery shop in Leechburg to replace his battery.

I'd gladly go over to get a break from writing and out of the house, even with the fresh snow and bitter cold. I secretly wanted to test out my all-wheel drive and studded snow tires. I listened to Quinn and Rose on my radio (104.7) in the car for the very short drive to the Colonel's. I remember Jim Quinn from when I was a kid, he was a DJ on the old B-94 radio station; he somehow transformed his image from a hip-hop DJ of the 1980s to a successful conservative talk show host that now was syndicated across the country along with several other radio talk show hosts like Rush Limbaugh, Glenn Beck, and Sean Hannity.

Though I did not always believe in everything Jim Quinn said, he was entertaining and informative. As usual, Quinn was complaining about some Democratic congressman's pork-barrel program and how the president's new energy bill would push jobs overseas. Just then, a news broadcast came on from Fox News, and this one broadcast would affect all six and a half billion of the world's population in less than three hours. Though, when first reported, it really did not get that much attention at all.

CHAPTER 3
Hectic Day at White House

> *"A continual atmosphere of hectic passion is very trying if you haven't got any of your own."*
> — Dorothy L. Sayers

"Good morning Mr. President," the aide said to President James (Jim) Stockwell as the commander in chief walked down the hall from his living quarters to the Oval Office, cup of coffee in hand.

It would be about an hour before the morning briefings. In the West Wing, various staff members were already working on their portion of the daily briefs to the president. National Security Director Chip Colby waited in the cafeteria, touching up his daily brief over a cup of coffee and a bagel. Chip would start the day off at 8:30 with President Stockwell's inner circle for the daily national security brief. Chip was a pro at this gig, with President Stockwell being the third president he had served under as national security director. All the major news channels, CNN, Fox, and MSNBC played in another West Wing office without anyone taking notice.

CNN started its lead plug at 8:30 with a story of two shooting stars—or something—directly over the North Pole, side by side. The story got no interest from the various aides who prepared the presidential briefs; they were scurrying about, caught in their own little world.

"Good morning, Mr. President, are you ready to go?" asked Chip, peeking into the Oval Office. He was one of the few who had full "walk in" privileges.

The daily brief started with the same daily spiels about Iran, Iraq, Russia, and Afghanistan. The president was used to these types of briefings, having served in the army for thirty-three years and retiring as a three-star general before becoming a congressman and then governor of Pennsylvania.

Chip said, "The National Security Office is closely monitoring the flu epidemic in Africa and South America," but the president was only half listening, sipping on his coffee.

"As of yet, the Center for Disease Control's scientists have not been able to isolate the bug's origin; it's like it came out of nowhere, Mr. President," said Chip, raising his voice to get the president's attention. "Though treatable with aggressive antibiotics, it can be a nasty bug that is highly contagious if left untreated," Chip read from his briefing notes, looking up to make eye contact from time to time. He concluded, "So far, the bug is affecting mainly the world's Southern Hemisphere; it is strange, though, Mr. President, with its origination point on two separate continents at the same time, and not in the Far East as is usually the case."

CHAPTER 4
Route 28 Blues

"Americans will put up with anything provided it doesn't block traffic."
Dan Rather

A lady in the next car looked over at Johnnie like he was nuts as he sang with animated gestures in the traffic jam. Just then, Johnnie's cell phone rang.

Johnnie answered his cell phone through his radio via Bluetooth. "Yes, Missy," he said as he abruptly stopped singing along to Jimmy Buffet's "Margaritaville." Johnnie hated the way Missy had a knack for calling him in the middle of one of his favorite songs; though now he tried extra hard to be patient with here. Missy had a "bun in the oven," as he liked to say.

"How are you doing, honey, where are you at?" asked Missy as Johnnie fought for his inches of progress on Route 28, just past the Tarentum exit.

"Not even to the Pittsburgh Mills yet," Johnnie said, putting his car into park to rest his leg.

Penn DOT decided to start construction of a new bridge over the Pennsylvania Turnpike on Route 28 in October 2011, only to not start work or remove the Jersey barriers, keeping this major artery to Pittsburgh to a single lane in both directions over the winter. Johnnie wondered how the Penn DOT management could do this, even when no work was going to be done. Today, all traffic was backed up further than normal due to a stalled car.

"I haven't moved a hundred feet in over an hour. Last week, I waited for ninety minutes as traffic slowly passed by a guy with a flat tire on my way home from work—and he was not even on the roadway," Johnnie joked. "I felt sorry for the poor bastard, as people scowled at him; some did worse, with hand and arm gestures," Johnnie said, half laughing.

Missy talked to Johnnie from the kitchen table, as the news played muted in the background on their 60-inch plasma television. The satellite receiver was only partially working, either because of the new snow on the dish or the dark snow clouds overhead.

"Don't forget Johnnie, I have a doctor visit tomorrow, I want you there to hear the baby's heartbeat," Missy said.

"Yes, honey," Johnnie said tenderly.

CHAPTER 5
The Graveyard Shift

"I put all my genius into my life; I put only my talent into my works."
OSCAR WILDE

At the Ground-based Electro Optical Deep Space Surveillance (GEODSS) observatory on top of Mount Haleakula, Hawaii, a lone airman dutifully watched over the sky at two a.m. local time. His job was to photograph the night sky and transmit the data back to Schriever Air Force Base in the desert east of Colorado Springs, for processing. The pictures this GEODSS site took, along with its sister GEODSS sites in both Spain and Diego Garcia in the Indian Ocean, tracked all the space debris in earth's orbit. Air Force Space Command used this three-dimensional charting to warn spacecraft of collision hazards with space junk. Even an object as small as a paint chip could crack a shuttle windshield when moving at 18,500 miles per hour.

Flicking his ash into a butt can near a lone silversword at the door, Airman Grotten shivered in the cool night air; he grabbed another smoke to stay awake. The GEODSS site was on the top of a 12,000-foot-high dormant volcano. Grotten was just about to step back inside when he looked up and saw what he thought were two shooting stars or planets—or something—to the extreme north, both brighter than all the other stars around them.

He went inside and took some more readings of the objects with the GEODSS telescope. *This can't be right* he said to himself. The objects were barely 60,000 miles from earth.

He sent the telemetry data to his counterparts in Colorado Springs. About thirty minutes later the duty officer, a Captain, asked him to get another set of readings on the objects. This time the objects were about 51,000 miles away. Also, Airman Grotten noticed that a tail was starting to form on both objects.

****

For most college students, a snow delay in college was a good thing. For the cadets at the Virginia Military Institute, a snow day meant marching extra drill in the trampled-down snow. House Mountain, normally visible from the VMI parade ground, was shrouded in a veil of clouds that day, even after the snow had stopped falling.

The cadet Regimental Commander for the Corps of Cadets Van Price worked his cadets hard. Cadet Price exuded absolute leadership. He was already serving in the army reserve and been through Ranger School; his father had served in Iraq, earning the Silver Star during Desert Storm, and his grandfather, an army veteran, served too—he died in Vietnam on his fourth tour of duty.

Old Gunnery Sergeant Frank Joyce inspected the ranks of cadets. Sergeant Joyce struck fear into the heart of every cadet, even the regimental commander. Joyce was tough as nails and hard-core. When the professors took the chance to come in late for classes with all the new snow, Gunny Joyce personally dug out his driveway of a foot of snow to have the chance to do more drill time with the cadets.

Cadet Price came to attention and smartly said, "Good morning, Gunnery Sergeant Joyce."

The Gunny Sergeant returned salutations, "Good morning, cadet regimental commander, is the corps of cadet ready for drill?"

Cadet Price had learned in his first days at the Institute not to call the Gunny Sergeant "sir." A cadet doing so would be verbally blasted by the sergeant: "Don't call me *sir*, I work for a God damned living!"

****

The Operations Center at Schriever Air Force Base, usually quiet at 5 a.m. Mountain Standard Time, was now a hub of activity. At the Cheyenne Mountain complex on the other side of Colorado Springs, at the foothills of the Rocky Mountains, the once Cold War command post for NORAD had sprung to life as well.

The Cheyenne Mountain complex duty officer of the day, Lt. Col. Keith Stanley said to the young enlisted woman at the console, "Get me in contact with the U.S. Space Command commander, General Hawk, ASAP!"

General Stephen (Steve) Hawk was out for his morning run on Peterson Air Force Base, in Colorado Springs. His aides were always within eyeshot, just a little out of earshot of their boss; they hated this part of the job, but it came with the territory.

"Major Bilco, get me General Hawk ASAP," said Lt. Col. Stanley to the general's aide on his secure cell phone.

"This better be good, Colonel Stanley, or it is your and my asses both on a platter, sir," said the major. He reluctantly approached the general with the cell phone.

"General Hawk, we have a situation, we are tracking two objects, apparently asteroids, on a collision track with earth," Stanley said calmly to the general over the hand set. "Sir, just look to your extreme north," Stanley said, knowing the general was on his morning run at Peterson AF Base.

The general dropped his cell phone from his ear and his aides scrambled to pick it up, fixing the battery case that fell off and handing it back to the general.

"Just how far away are they?" General Hawk asked once he got the phone to his ear.

"About 38,000 miles now from earth, sir," said the Lieutenant Colonel.

"Jesus, Keith, how could we have not seen them sooner!" barked the general.

"The asteroids have the oddest track, sir, coming almost straight down on the North Pole; these rocks do not follow the normal orbital plane other planets and asteroids do in our solar system; they are not consistent with comets' orbital tracks, either," Stanley went on to say. "If you ever wanted to keep them hidden until the last moment, this is the track you'd use, sir."

"How long do we have until these hit, Keith?" the general reluctantly asked, not really wanting to know the answer.

"About two hours, sir, probably a little less," Stanley said, his voice quivering as he tried to swallow.

"What are the masses of these two objects?" asked the general.

Lt. Col. Stanley handed the phone to an aide, who took over with a technical explanation of the asteroids' masses.

"One asteroid is approximately six miles wide, and the other about a mile wide; we estimate the larger object will hit first in the Pacific Ocean about 500 miles south of the Aleutian Islands, and the smaller object will hit in the Atlantic ocean about twenty minutes later, less than 100 miles west of England," the NORAD officer said matter-of-factly.

"How could we have missed this? Damn it!" the general barked again to the anonymous aide standing too close to him. "Get me the president ASAP! Also conference in the secretary of defense, they should be starting their morning briefings in DC by now," the general added. He had been a White House aide early in his career.

"Keith, get another team working with NASA to validate our data, and a third to assess the effect these asteroids will have on the earth, if they strike the earth as we project they will," ordered General Hawk, a hint of stress now in his voice. "I want this done yesterday!"

"Yes sir, already started," Stanley said.

The aide called for a Blackhawk chopper to transport General Hawk from the Peterson AFB flight line to the Cheyenne Mountain NORAD bunker on the other side of Colorado Springs; they would not have time to get him to the mountain through the normal Colorado Springs morning traffic.

CHAPTER 6
Chaos

"Chaos is the score upon which reality is written."
HENRY MILLER

"Good morning Colonel," I said, as Dad met me at the car, getting the door. "I just heard on the radio of some kind of alert about a shooting star or something," I said.

Without saying anything, the Colonel got my wheelchair out and brought it around to the driver's-side door for me; the Colonel had built wheelchair ramps into the house when we first moved here after his time in the army. Knowing I was already coming to help the Colonel with his truck battery, Mom made breakfast for the two of us. The smell of bacon wafted through the old farm house as it sizzled on the griddle.

I saw the table was already set, with real maple syrup for the pancakes, and fresh coffee. The Colonel and I went into the living room and turned on CNN. The screen showed a reporter, with the top right corner showing some kind of shooting star. Not quite registering what was going on, I turned up the volume.

"For those of you that just joined us, we are tracking two apparent meteors, possibly comets, above the North Pole," the reporter said, holding his finger to his ear, trying to get some new info from the off-camera feed. "At this time, we do not know if they are a danger or not," the reporter went on to say.

"Wait," he then said. He held his finger to his ear again.

"We just got word that Marine One landed on the White House lawn and that all news crews were asked to leave the White House grounds immediately." The reporter looked confused.

"From what we know, the president was not scheduled to go anywhere today, what with the signing of his historic energy independence bill," the newsman said, but his face said that something was not right with this report.

"This is really peculiar behavior, what do you think is going on, Colonel?" I asked him.

"I don't know, Rege," the Colonel said, as we listened to the news.

The Colonel then abruptly walked out of the living room and into his study.

****

A Secret Service man burst through the door of the Oval Office and said, "Mr. President, we need to get you out of Washington right now."

"I don't understand, let me talk to the agent in charge," President Stockwell demanded.

"Mr. President, I'll tell you as we are walking," the agent in charge said, meeting him just outside the door.

"We are tracking two asteroids on a collision course with earth," the agent finally said.

"How?" asked the president.

"They showed up over the North Pole from the outer solar system; they are coming in at such an unlikely angle we never even saw them coming until this morning, maybe an hour ago, when they appeared visually," the agent said as he almost physically dragged the president down the hall.

"One in a trillion is an understatement when calculating the odds of something like this happening from this trajectory," the agent said, paraphrasing what the White House science advisor had said to him only moments earlier.

"Where are we going?" asked the president.

"We are taking you to Site R in Pennsylvania; it's an old bunker facility—"

"I know where it is at and its purpose," said Stockwell, cutting the agent off in mid-sentence. "Why there, though?" asked the President.

"We estimate if the one asteroid hits as projected, there will be a tsunami wave that will inundate the entire eastern seaboard. We estimate a 1,000-foot wave will overrun Washington DC, rendering the bunker below the White House ineffective," the agent said. "We do not have time to get you to the NORAD bunker in Colorado. And Mr. President, Europe, Western Africa, and South America will also be hit by the same tsunami as Washington from the projected European strike," the agent said, exiting the door to the south lawn.

"And the other asteroid, where will it hit?"

"It will actually hit first, by 22 minutes, in the Pacific Ocean near Alaska", the agent said.

"That is the one that will cause the real harm to the earth," said the agent as he talked into his sleeve, trying to give some type of status. Then, trying to expedite things, the agent said, "We can go over the details, sir, once we get you airborne on Marine One. We are almost out of time."

CHAPTER 7
Safety

"Safety is something that happens between your ears, not something you hold in your hands."
JEFF COOPER

The president boarded Marine One with the Secret Service agent in charge, and Chip walked in behind him. As if reading the president's mind, the agent said, "Someone will be getting your wife" as they waited in the chopper.

They could not hear each other talking over the whining of the helicopter's auxiliary power unit with the chopper door still open. The President did not see the press set up on the White House lawn as he normally did. A minute later, the First Lady emerged from the White House, being almost forced to run to the chopper.

"What about my daughters at Pepperidge High School?" asked the president.

"We'll send someone for them," the agent responded.

"The hell you will—we'll pick them up on the way," the president ordered with an almost scary look in his eyes.

"Sir, we can't do that," the agent explained.

"I'm not leaving Washington unless we pick up my daughters along the way, national emergency or not—that is an order," the president demanded.

The Secret Service chief relented and whispered something into the device in his sleeve, and Marine One took off from the White House lawn. The president and First Lady looked out the window as they cleared the White House grounds, and they could now see the two asteroids in the northern sky, even in broad daylight, with the tails trailing far behind them. Seeing the asteroids for themselves, they both somehow knew now that time was short.

****

The Colonel got off the phone with one of his old contacts at Pennsylvania National Guard headquarters; his face had lost all its color. He then said in the most matter-of-fact voice, "Call Kaitlin and tell her to get over here now—do what I said, don't hesitate. Just call her!"

I have never seen the Colonel ever act like this before in his life, I thought. He looked scared.

The Colonel was never the one for theatrics; he was and is the most cool, calm, and collected person I have ever known in my life. I pulled out my cell phone and called Kaitlin. "She's going to think I've lost my mind, Colonel," I said, waiting for the phone to ring.

I told her to come to the Colonel's house right away. She was miffed by it all. However, the daycare center had only a couple kids due to the snow and the owner had asked her earlier if she wanted to go home.

The Colonel said, "Is she was driving yet"? The Colonel then said, "Put her on speaker on your cell."

"Listen, Kaitlin, this is Bob, I just heard from my friend at the Pennsylvania National Guard headquarters that there are two asteroids about to impact with the earth in less than one hour. You need to get to my house, I have a place we can go." The Colonel was keeping his cool.

I broke in to say, "Kaitlin, I'm watching the news on TV about the shooting stars, and it's on all the radio stations now."

"I want you to call your sister and Johnnie and tell them to get to my house," the Colonel said, taking over the conversation. "I may have a place we can be safe until this thing passes over."

"Okay, Colonel, I'll call Missy and Johnnie," Kaitlin said, starting to realize the gravity of the situation.

****

A young "rat" on guard duty came running onto the VMI parade field and headed straight for Gunny Joyce. The rat whispered something into the sergeant's ear. They looked skyward to the north. Then Gunny Sergeant yelled out to all the cadets, "Change into full combat gear and bring your ruck sacks with full canteens and rations to the cadet chapel in fifteen minutes! I need everyone moving double time!"

Even for the Institute, this was an odd set of orders, but the cadets complied without question.

****

Marine One touched down at the Pepperidge High School football field in Arlington, Virginia. The girls' Secret Service agents loaded Jamie and Emma Stockwell onto the chopper and it took off again after being on the ground no more than a minute. Crowds of students watched while all of this transpired in front of them, not realizing the helpless state they were actually in themselves.

"What's going on, Daddy?" both of the president's daughters seemed to ask in unison.

"I'll tell you soon," he said, "but not right now. How long to Site R?" he asked the agent.

"It'll take us about thirty-five minutes to get there," the agent answered smartly, having already anticipated the question.

The president could tell that Marine One was being pushed to it maximum for speed by the excessive whine of the engine and the bumpiness of the ride.

"Mr. President, as I was saying, the asteroid that will hit the Pacific is the real problem," the agent in charge said. "It is over six miles wide, about the same size as the asteroid that hit the Yucatan Peninsula and took out the dinosaurs sixty-five million years ago, and we think it will cause a firestorm fifteen thousand plus miles in every direction from ground zero." The president's daughters listened in on the conversation.

"What the firestorm does not destroy outright will subsequently get roasted," the agent elaborated.

"What are you trying to say?" asked the president.

"Mr. President, your science advisor says that the ejecta from the strikes, mainly the Pacific strike, will rain down on the earth for the next forty-eight hours, raising the air temperature to over 400 degrees Fahrenheit." Everyone on the chopper listened intently. "After the heat wave passes, the smoke and ash will block out the sun for about fifteen months, throwing the world into complete darkness and dropping the median temperature to below freezing for well over a year. Once the smoke and dust in the atmosphere clear, the temperature will be ten degrees higher than pre-impact averages around the globe for centuries to come, until it dissipates, causing global warming on a scale not seen in recorded history."

"How do we warn the masses?" asked the President.

"There's not much we can do sir, honestly," Chip said, taking over the conversation from the Secret Service agent. "Unless a person is underground, and not just in a basement, they will not be alive twelve hours from now," he said with a lump in his throat. "One more piece of bad news, sir," Chip said, trying to break the info into smaller pieces.

"What more could there possibly be?" the president inquired, looking visibly angry now.

"There will be an electromagnetic pulse shock wave from the Pacific impact which will essentially knock out every electronic device on the planet in about forty minutes," Chip said, looking at his watch. "Unless an electronic device is EMP-hardened, it will be rendered useless", reported Chip.

The president's daughters were now both crying. The president's wife was visibly upset as well. President Stockwell was well aware of EMP danger, having recently read William Forstchen's novel *One Second After*, about an EMP attack on America. "Jesus, what options do we have?" asked the president, looking for anything to grab onto.

"Not really any, Mr. President, we estimate that this event will kill well over six billion of the earth's people, and that, sir, is honestly being optimistic. About 500,000 humans will be alive tomorrow at this time, mainly military lucky enough to already be in bunkers and some survivalists types in Montana and Utah, some Swiss, and some of our submarines in the Southern Hemisphere," Chip said as he was reading something from his BlackBerry.

The chopper set down in the parking lot at Site R. Snow blew up from the unplowed lot, as the chopper's wheels touched the ground. There was no fanfare, as the first family quickly got off the chopper and were ushered inside the Site R facility.

****

"Missy, this is Kaitlin," she said as Missy answered her cell phone. "Did you see the news?" Kaitlin asked as she drove down the New Schenley Road. "I need you to come to Regis's dad's house", Kaitlin said, putting the cell phone on speaker. She went on, "I do not have time to explain, you will just have to trust me on this one—something very bad is going to happen with these asteroids that are on the news right now".

"Are they going to hit the earth?" Missy asked meekly.

"You need to call Johnnie and tell him to go to the Colonel's house as quick as he can," Kaitlin said calmly. "The Colonel has a cave over the hill from his house where we can stay to ride things out."

"Ok" Missy said, "I am walking to my car now, I'll call Johnnie as soon as I am moving."

Fumbling with her cell phone, and almost losing control of her car in the snow, Missy tried calling Johnnie's BlackBerry, but "All circuits busy, please try again later" was all she heard.

The radio made the screechy alert sound from the Emergency Broadcast System, which repeated several times. The announcer finally said, "An asteroid impact is imminent. All hearing this alert need to take shelter underground now."

The announcer then said, "The first impact will occur in eight minutes."

Johnnie heard the announcement as he turned up the radio. He tried calling Missy. "All circuits are busy," the automated phone message said. Johnnie was stuck in a traffic nightmare, and twenty-five miles from home; he may as well have been a million miles.

Just then, fire whistles rang out with the air raid signal used many years ago.

****

Kaitlin sped into the Colonel's driveway. The Colonel was waiting at the door for her. "Did you get ahold of Missy?" he inquired.

"Yes, she is driving here as we speak."

"Did she get ahold of Johnnie?"

"I do not know," was all Kaitlin could say. She pulled out her cell phone and tried calling Missy, and then Johnnie, but she also got the all-busy message. Kaitlin started to panic as she heard the numerous sirens now blaring from the various towns in the area.

The Colonel said, "Let's get inside the house and out of the cold for a moment, Kaitlin," as he took her arm. Kaitlin and the Colonel went into his study. He had this odd-looking phone in there. It was left over from his Army National Guard days, and still connected to the Military Defense Switched Network which had priority precedence capability. This feature was an override, able to make connections by preempting other telephone lines.

"What's Johnnie's cell number?" the Colonel asked Kaitlin. She gave him the number; he first dialed some numbers, then Johnnie's cell number; but the call did not go through, the line was busy.

****

Missy was now screaming, as she heard the alert on CNN. She was still trying desperately to call Johnnie. She got so flustered, she ran off the Old Schenley Road into a snow bank coming down the big hill. "Damn it!" she yelled, frantically pounding the steering wheel.

She was still a mile and a half from the Colonel's house. The tires just spun as she tried to back out. The alert came on the radio again, with the same message, only this time the announcer said, "The impact will to occur in the Pacific Ocean in two more minutes."

Missy's car would not budge. She screamed again.

****

At the chapel, Gunny Joyce told the cadets go to downstairs in an orderly fashion, by company. In the basement, which served also as the Stonewall Jackson Museum, Gunny Joyce took the boards off a wall near a display of old uniforms. Miffed by this time, Regimental Commander Van Price asked the Gunny

Sergeant, "What is going on, Gunnery Sergeant?" All this seemed so out of character, something the Gunny would never dream of doing under normal circumstances.

The Gunny said, "The earth is going to be impacted with an asteroid any moment. I am going to have the cadets go into the old tunnel complex built under the parade ground during the Civil War."

Joyce got every last cadet in the tunnels and closed the doors. Cadet flashlights broke through the darkness; their breaths steamed in the cold air. The Gunny then ordered the cadet regimental commander to have his cadet company commanders take a roll call and report back to him. Van Price ensured that the order was carried out expeditiously.

****

President Stockwell watched a CNN news feed in the Site R command center about the asteroid over the Pacific. It was still supposed to be dark on Maui, but the light coming from the asteroid made it now look like daylight. Time seemed to move in slow motion for the president. Staff members were yelling things, giving him all kinds of info, too much for one person to absorb, even for the president of the United States.

****

The astronauts on the International Space Station unwillingly had a front-row seat to the events unfolding below them, but they were completely helpless to intervene. They were told to shut everything down they could except for emergency life support, before the EMP shock wave hit. The space station was set up for solar flares affecting the electronics, but not EMP from asteroids.

Astronaut Dick Ford looked down on earth as it rotated beneath them. As they moved through their orbit, they saw the asteroid only minutes from impact. The object over the Pacific Ocean appeared like a large star with a long tail stretching thousand of miles behind it. The plume glowed in the sunlight.

"One minute to impact!" called out another astronaut from down one of the portals.

****

Johnnie's cell phone rang, masked though it was by the sirens. Johnnie only noticed because the light lit up as well with an unfamiliar number; then the Colonel came on the line.

"Johnnie, listen to me, its Bob Steele, I may have only a few seconds," the Colonel said. Johnnie struggled to hear him over the din of the chaos. "You need to get to my house; I have a cave 500 feet right behind the house, down over the hillside, and Missy, Kaitlin, Regis, my wife and I will be there. There is a steel door covering the cavern's entrance; when you get there, bang on the door three times and repeat," said the Colonel. "Do you understand, Johnnie?"

"Yes, Colonel, I do," Johnnie exclaimed over the noise.

"Where are you right now?" the Colonel inquired.

"I am on Route 28 near the Tarentum exit," Johnnie said, holding a finger over his other ear to block out the noise.

Just then, the phone connection cut out in mid-sentence.

****

Missy put her Jeep Liberty in four-wheel drive and the vehicle came out of the ditch, snow shooting up from all four wheels. She was moving again with less than two minutes until impact. She tried calling Johnnie and Kaitlin again, but with no luck. Just then, both the phone and her Jeep Liberty just went dead near a farm house. All the sirens stopped wailing and there was absolute quiet. Missy tried starting the Jeep Liberty, but it was as if there was no battery power. She just pounded on the dashboard as she screamed. Her cell phone wouldn't light up, either.

Missy was still about a mile from the Colonel's. The asteroid had impacted the earth. *Am I going to make it?* she wondered. *Is Johnnie?*

CHAPTER 8
Impact

"Life changes whether we like it or not."
ANONYMOUS

The electricity abruptly went out in the Colonels farm house. "Oh my God, Where's Missy and Johnnie?" Kaitlin said out to no one in particular at the kitchen table.

The Colonel said calmly, "Let's start getting everyone down to the cave now."

"What about Missy and Johnnie?" Kaitlin asked frantically.

"If Missy was on her way, she must be close, I'll look for her once I have you, Regis, and Emma in the cave," the Colonel said in a commanding voice. He then wheeled me down over the hill to the cave, almost crashing my wheelchair several times in the process.

As we went over the hill, the thing that amazed me most was the absolute silence, when minutes before there had been absolute chaos with all the sirens. The last time I recalled a silence of this magnitude was the evening of September 11, 2001, when the Colonel and I sat at the pavilion by his pond, just after Kaitlin and I came home that night from Maryland. I realized the silence now was because no airplanes were flying, and no cars were running on Route 28 or across the river.

WITHOUT WARNING

****

Johnnie tried starting his car, but even the dome light would not light up in it. Even if he could have gotten his car started, he would not have been able to drive anywhere with all the other cars in one massive jam. Johnnie stepped out of his car and pondered his predicament.

The silence was broken by other car doors opening and closing around him on Route 28, with people asking, "What's going on?"

Some people were dressed in suits, skirts, and other attire not suited for being outside for long in the cold. Johnnie caught something out of the corner of his eye as he looked up just in time toward the Tarentum Bridge. At that moment, a jet airliner rammed into the bridge and broke up in the Allegheny River. Apparently, the airplane's engines had gone out in midflight. Johnnie's military instincts kicked in and he took inventory of the situation. He was at least twenty miles from home or the Colonel's house. An asteroid had impacted just a few minutes ago over the Pacific and another was due to strike in the Atlantic Ocean any minute. Radio emergency personnel said to get underground. He watched as more folks emerged from their cars, realizing their cars were not going to start again. Then he thought, *I must get underground. Sewers? Probably not.*

With more than a foot of snow on the ground, it would not be good if things started melting. He looked up, and it hit him like a ton of bricks: the Tour-Ed Mine. It was an old coal mine now used for tours. Johnnie said to the other people around him, "Let's head for the mine up on the hill."

But no one paid him any attention. They just started walking toward Tarentum. Johnnie took off up the hill alone for the old coal mine, about a half mile away.

****

The Colonel found Missy running down the Sportsman Road towards his house. Her voice resonated in the absolute silence. Just about breathless, and almost in shock, she said she could not get hold of Johnnie.

The Colonel said, "I got through to him using his military phone line and told him to come to the cave," but this didn't help much to calm her down.

They both ran to the cave. The Colonel showed her inside, then ran back to his barn and grabbed thirteen hens and three roosters and then about ten Pekin ducks, some mallard ducks just in case things got hairy. The Colonel then went back for five sheep, and several loads of feed. He put the chickens and ducks in burlap bags, then let them go in the cave. Same with the sheep. He would sort it all out later.

****

Most of the cadets in the tunnels under the VMI parade ground had no idea yet why they were there. With 800 cadets squeezed into an area made for half that number of people, the tunnel system was claustrophobic and the air was hard to breathe. The cadets settled into the larger openings by company. Rumors ran rampant as to why this was all happening.

****

The astronauts watched in horror as the asteroid hit the Pacific Ocean, though not a sound was made in the vacuum of space. The light from the impact was brighter than the sun, temporarily blinding everyone. As the light dissipated, a mushroom cloud emerged, going up into the stratosphere, with large pieces of debris shooting out like fireworks in all directions. The clouds instantly dissolved 1,000 miles in every direction from the impact site.

It was agonizing watching the firestorm consuming everything outwards from the impact site from the heat generated at the impact point. When the firestorm hit land, it consumed all in its path, everything just spontaneously combusted. The West Coast ignited, then what appeared to be Colorado, then on towards Kansas, then Missouri and just about to Ohio—all was consumed by flames. The firestorm seemed to finally fizzle out in the heavy clouds over the East Coast.

The astronauts watched as the second asteroid impacted the ocean near Europe twenty minutes later. The firestorm seemed to stretch about a thousand miles in all directions, consuming most of Europe. As the space station crossed over Russia, Dick could see the wrath on the backside of the firestorm over a lot of Russia, China, Korea, and Japan from the Pacific strike. Both the Russian and Chinese astronauts looked in horror at the devastation of their homelands.

****

Because the catacombs under the parade ground had no electricity running to them, the cadets were initially oblivious to the power failure caused by the EMP. They say leaders are brokers in hope, and Regimental Commander Van Price did not fail that day. He did an outstanding job to carve order out of all the chaos, barking out order after order, and his fellow cadets worked hard to heed and comply. Gunny Joyce stood in the background in awe as Cadet Van Price commanded at his best.

****

"Mr. President, we lost the majority of the communications from Site R to the outside world," Chip reported to the president. "We do have a couple lines open to NORAD at Cheyenne Mountain that are EMP protected; all they could relate are that the asteroids impacted and all communications to Peterson and

Schriever Air Force Bases have now ceased," Chip said. "NORAD says they do have communications to a few missile locations and a handful of nuclear submarines in the Southern Hemisphere on the low bands, and that is about it."

They were sitting in the communications room. Chip went on, "If our estimations are correct, the shock wave from the Pacific impact will hit us in approximately ninety minutes, Mr. President."

****

Johnnie climbed up the hill to the Tour-Ed Mine; he heard another plane go down somewhere further in the distance a few minutes later; he was not exactly sure where it was, though, possibly Lower Burrell by the sound of it. He also swore he heard gunshots down on Route 28. He wondered if civilization could break down this fast.

The Tour-Ed Mine sign read: Closed for the Season.

Johnnie grabbed a pick ax that was part of a coal car display in the parking lot and busted down the door to the admissions building. The entrance to the mine shaft connected to it. Johnnie sat down about a hundred or so feet into the mine, his eyes adjusting to the few battery-powered lights cutting through the darkness. The air was warm compared to outside, but still a cool fifty-two degrees when compared to normal room temperature. It had been almost an hour since the impact.

Not too bad, the power went out, and planes are falling from the sky, but nothing else, Johnnie thought.

****

The Colonel locked the door to the cave behind him after he brought down one more load of supplies from the barn. The electricity in the cave still worked off its battery power, but the lights seemed excessively dim compared to normal lighting. The

Colonel had just walked up to Pap's cabin inside the cave when the shock wave hit. The outside door of the cave sounded like a train or a tornado passed by it. The cave door buckled and groaned but held. Kaitlin, Missy, and Mom all just screamed from the din of the shock wave. Everyone's ears popped with the pressure change.

****

Johnnie was just about to go back out of the mine when the shock wave hit. The entrance building's windows shattered from the concussion. The suction of the wind popped Johnnie's ears badly; he ran even deeper in the cave out of instinct. As the shockwave roared by the people standing on Route 28, almost every one of them had their eardrums burst from the force of the concussion. Surprisingly, emergency lights were still on in the Tour-Ed Mine; they must have automatically come on when the external power cut out from the EMP pulse.

Near one of the lights, there was a survival room display. Johnnie found a flashlight with a crank recharger and went into the survival room. The room had real food, clothing, cots, sleeping bags, and pads, along with a lot of other survival gear. As Johnnie sat there in the display vestibule, all he could think about was his wife, Missy, and their unborn child.

****

When the shock wave hit Site R, no one could even tell; they were deep underground in a hermetically sealed bunker. Above ground, Marine One and all the other cars in the parking lot had their windows cracked with some of them shattering.

"We estimate it'll be about four hours until the tsunami hits the East Coast from the European strike," an aide said to the president and Chip. "Secondary debris will start falling any time now for approximately the next thirty-five to forty hours. The biggest pieces of debris will fall closest to the impact locations. The finer particulates of ejecta will fall worldwide, causing the earth's atmosphere to rise to over 400 degrees for the next forty hours as well as causing secondary firestorms from combustibles spontaneously igniting."

"Do we have any climate data available yet?" asked the president to the crew permanently stationed at Site R.

"All we know so far is that the surface temperature is now already fifty-two degrees, up from twenty-five degrees two hours ago, pre-impact," said an aide feeling almost helpless relating the trickle of information to the president.

"It's about noon, I would have signed my energy independence bill by now," the president murmured to himself.

"Instead, everything in this world has changed so drastically in the last three hours that it may be decades, centuries, eons, and maybe even never before things get back to some type of normalcy." He was rambling. "What can be normal anymore?" the president said, putting his hands on his forehead.

CHAPTER 9

A Bad Day for the Earth

"I have long considered it one of God's greatest mercies that the future is hidden from us. If it were not, life would surely be unbearable."
UNKNOWN

The people of Cocoa Beach, Florida, wandered around dazed and confused from the shockwave that had roared past them two hours earlier. Cars had stopped in their place on the intercoastal causeway as their electronic ignitions died from the EMP pulse. Father Joe Greenidge was on his way from his parish office in Cape Canaveral to the diocese headquarters in Orlando for a meeting when he got stranded on Route 522, in the middle of the causeway bridge near Merritt Island. He only heard bits and pieces of what was happening from the radio before it died. The sky was now starting to turn an eerie dark red hue.

He could see Cocoa Beach behind him, with Merritt Island in the other direction. The padre then heard a grinding sound in the distance, and a large cruise ship at Port Canaveral started leaning sideways as the water in the inlet drained out of the port. But nothing surprised him now—he had seen three planes fall out of the sky earlier, just after the power went out and his car died.

The priest looked back over to Cocoa Beach and a sight that was almost surreal. It looked like a wall of water over 1,000 feet high was coming. The wall of water towered over the tallest buildings on the Cocoa Beach and Cape Canaveral coastlines. Father Joe said one last Hail Mary and made a sign of the cross as the water hit him. The wall of water kept going, covering the entire breadth of the state of Florida and into the Gulf of Mexico. This scene repeated itself on the coastlines and low-lying areas all around the world. By 5 p.m. Eastern Standard Time, every shoreline was hit by at least one tsunami, and many were hit by repeat sets of waves.

****

The cadets closest to the tunnel door felt the air pressure change from the shock wave. Gunny Sergeant Joyce attempted to check the status outside; the heat, he knew, was already becoming intolerable. In the tunnel, Van Price had to deal with issue after issue. The Gunny, thinking ahead, charged some cadets with digging a latrine in one of the back caverns. Not knowing how long the corps of cadets would be in the underground tunnels, Van Price charged his company commanders with working a plan to ration the water, food, and even the flashlight batteries they had on hand.

****

By five o'clock the sky had turned a dark blood red, with the ejecta starting to fall back to earth. The temperature in Buenos Aries was now over 150 degrees Fahrenheit and rising. People tried hiding in their basements—to no avail. Some people took to the sewers and found some relief. The temperature was over 270 degree in Zimbabwe by 9 p.m. All people and animals above ground had been dead for several hours.

In Leechburg, Pennsylvania, the temperature was over 350 degrees at 11 p.m. on the day of the impacts. The foot of snow had long since melted, with torrential boiling rain now falling from the vaporized oceans. The streams overflowed their banks from the downpours. The drainage systems were overwhelmed with snow melt and rain and forced folks that had taken refuge in them back out into the heat.

The Allegheny River was now higher than at any previously recorded flood level: docks, boats, barges, and houses started flowing downstream in a cataclysmic swirl. No human above ground was alive to see the carnage. Less than thirteen hours earlier, the Allegheny River had been completely frozen; its water was now hotter than a tub of steaming bath water.

Upriver, water started flowing over top of the dam at Kinzua about 11:35 p.m. On top of the dam, all kinds of debris jammed the intake spillways, blocking the water's exit from the dam. Water overtook the earthen part of the dam and flowed over the side. At one in the morning, Kinzua Dam broke. A wall of water now flowed unrestrained down the Allegheny River valley with nothing to hinder it, taking out town after town along the way. The rumbling of the water sounded like 10,000 locomotive trains all running at once.

To get away from the heat, a few fortunate souls, some with blood still running from their ears as a result of the shock wave, took refuge in the underground drainage system in Kittanning. But they soon perished as a 100-foot-high released from the Kinzua Dam came rushing down the Allegheny River and into the Ohio River. All low-span bridges above Kittanning, Pennsylvania immediately washed out, as well as numerous bridges on the Allegheny River's tributaries, with the widespread flooding. The high-span bridge for Route 28/422 over the Allegheny River near Ford City held.

The Crooked Creek dam held, but immense amounts of water flowed through the emergency overflow. Every other bridge south of Ford City down to Pittsburgh was washed away, less the Washington crossing bridge. Almost every bridge on the Conamaugh River in Johnstown, Pennsylvania, connecting to the

Kiskiminetas River, washed away as well. The carnage from the flooding made the famous Johnstown Flood of 1899 look like a light rain. The smell of smoke, waterlogged earth, and death permeated the entire valley. A large sign from the Congressman John Murtha hospital in Johnstown lodged at the top of the bridge in Leechburg. The din of the water flowing unrestrained sounded like Niagara Falls.

****

In the cabin inside the cave, the entire Steele family, and Missy, huddled in a small room with lots of maps around a table. The air smelled like kerosene fuel that burned in the little kerosene space heater. Just then, the ground rumbled as the wall of water from Kinzua Dam passed through the valley below them.

"What's that noise, Colonel?" asked Kaitlin, with quivering voice and absolute terror in her eyes.

"I don't know, probably an earthquake, I'm not sure," he said as the candles shook on the flimsy card table. Everyone huddled together in the little structure in the middle of the cave. The Colonel said the Lords Prayer and they all held hands in the little room.

Missy was in shock; she had resigned herself to the idea that Johnnie was already dead. She saw the remote outside thermometer go to 130 degrees; it would not go any higher. The Colonel then disconnected the sensor prong to save the thermometer. The steel door to the outside was so hot you could not even get close to it.

****

In the mine, Johnnie heard a roar outside that sounded like a runaway locomotive; he had grown immune to the din of the catastrophe, but this sound was something different. Ever the tactician, Johnnie made a mental note of all the supplies in the mine; there was enough food and water for a month, easily, as well as clothing, albeit mining attire.

The main obstacle Johnnie faced now was absolute boredom, and not knowing if his wife was alive—and of course the waiting for whatever was happening outside to pass. *Would it pass?* he wondered.

Only time would tell, and Johnnie's digital watch did not work anymore. He would just have to wait it out in the mine. Time was such a hard thing to gauge with no frame of reference. Johnnie lay down on a miner's cot.

****

Some of the staff at Site R finally started to take a rest. It was 2 a.m. of day two. The new morning would not bring solace however, they discovered when they woke up. All the staff had lost loved ones in the catastrophe. The president had now been up for over twenty-four hours straight. With the dark circles under his eyes, and a look of just plain tiredness in his face, President Stockwell looked like he had been up for over a week. The only communications he had to the outside world, at this point, was with NORAD at the Cheyenne Mountain complex on the EMP-resistant network.

With the gigantic steel doors of the compound sealed tight, the personnel at Cheyenne Mountain had no information now on what was going on right outside the mountain area, much less anywhere else in the world. They had lost all communications except for the single link to Site R. The president wondered if the Russian premier or any other of the world's leaders were still even alive at this point.

Mrs. Stockwell finally ordered her husband to come to bed and get some sleep. She got a sedative from the site's doctor for him. As he lay down in one of the only private rooms, he still could not completely grasp what had happened in the last twenty-eight hours. He fell asleep holding his wife in his arms.

****

By Thursday, February 9, 2012, the larger ejecta had finally fallen back to the ground and the smaller debris still rained down, keeping the surface temperature well over 300 degrees. Astronaut Dick Ford now looked out of his window at the grayed-out earth below him. The surface features of the planet were unrecognizable through the thick clouds of smoke and dust. The smoke blocked the entire planet from view. Cloud structures that looked like hurricanes perpetually calved from the Pacific impact zone, only to blend into the gray abyss several thousand miles away.

****

Johnnie could feel the heat getting unbearable long before he could even get close to the mine entrance. Though he could not tell, it had been twenty-five hours since the impacts. Johnnie passed the time doodling on the mine inspection log sheets; he used this time to recall different periods of his life in detail. He felt he finally had a real perspective of what a prisoner serving life in solitary confinement might feel. What kept Johnnie going was the hope Missy was still alive at the Colonel's cave. If anyone could pull it off, Johnnie knew the Colonel could find a way; that man did not have the word fail in his vocabulary. Johnnie was not too far from that mark himself.

****

The Colonel woke me up at about 10 a.m. on day two. I don't think I fell asleep until five. Time has lost all meaning to me now, anyhow. It had been a little over a day now, and it already seemed like an eternity. My watch stopped working with the impact, though I kept it on my wrist in the hope all would go back to normal, but this was a big mistake. The Colonel, being the military man he was, and in a lot of tough situations, started firing on all eight cylinders just about then, and we all desperately needed his leadership. The Colonel did not fail.

He tasked me to inventory every last supply we had in the cave, and especially to figure out how long our food supplies would last, as well as to make a consumption plan. He tasked Kaitlin and Missy to set up three living areas in the little cabin in the cave; one for the Colonel and Mom, one for Kaitlin and me, and one for Missy and Johnnie. No one said it, but we all doubted Johnnie was still alive. However, this was one reality none of us were quite ready to face yet.

The Colonel had Mom go through all the clothing to see what she could salvage or use in some manner. He organized the radio room Pap had set up into a pseudo-command post; he had already marked on the map the approximate locations of the impacts. Pap had several old-time radios with vacuum tubes that the Colonel started to look at and organize. Pap also had a large collection of survival, how-to, and medical books, plus a complete set of Encyclopedia Britannicas, albeit from 1973, and of course a hardcover King James Bible.

Besides taking inventory of all the supplies, today was the day I officially started my journal of my family's ordeals and experiences. If we actually did survive all this, it may be worth noting our trials and tribulations.

****

Dick Ford had the same idea of taking inventory of stocks at the International Space Station. The shuttle had left two weeks before, and brought four months of supplies for the crew of eight. However, Ford estimated that with the plentitude of supplies already on board, and a now fully functional garden and water reuse system, the crew could stay aloft for about two years living on a limited calorie diet. With the large greenhouse pod recently installed, the air would get stale but would retain breathable levels of oxygen. The plan could work if there were no surprises. The one thing for certain about space—there were a lot of surprises; and Dick Ford knew that.

CHAPTER 10
The Cool Down

"If global cooling will come soon, scientists will lose trust."
SHIGENORI MARUYAMA

Approximately forty-eight hours had passed since the two impacts. The Colonel put his hand on the cave entrance door; the metal had cooled significantly. He opened the door ever so slightly and felt the rush of hot air hit him like opening an oven door. Though terribly hot outside, the temperature was within human tolerances. The Colonel suspected it was about 100 degrees; when he hooked up the thermometer again, it was not too far off from his estimate, with the thermometer reading 103 degrees.

The sky was absolute pitch black at about 8 a.m. The Colonel swore he saw lightning or something else lighting the sky from time to time when he peered out the cave entrance. Although he could not see it, the Allegheny River below sounded more like a raging cataclysm than a tamed river managed by the Army Corps of Engineers. The wind blew about thirty mph and felt like a hair dryer blowing on his face. From the light of his flashlight, everything appeared soot-covered in the immediate area.

The Colonel and Kaitlin then stepped out of the cave and walked up over the hill from the cave to the Colonel's house.

The shockwave from the impact appeared to have blown out every window in the house. The Colonel wiped the dripping sweat from his brow, peering at the targets of his flashlight beam. Trees branches as well as other debris littered the yard for as far as he could see in the flashlight's beam. All the animals in the barn lay dead, and stank.

The Colonel motioned for Kaitlin to head to the house; it was hard to hear each other over the din of the gusty wind and raging river, perpetual noises that overpowered their voices. Kaitlin noticed all the candles on the kitchen table had melted from the extreme heat. Water gushed out of the freezer when the Colonel opened it; it also had a most putrid smell that hit the Colonel like a fist.

Sweating profusely from the extreme heat, they started collecting as many supplies as they could gather, mainly canned goods, which they loaded into large garbage bags. The Colonel went in another room and brought in several military A-bags, and he had three rifles slung over his shoulder. With the heat almost intolerable now, the two loaded as much as they could into a wheelbarrow from the garage and headed back down to the cave.

****

Johnnie awoke from a restless sleep. He had attempted to lie down to rest on the miner's cot but never slept for more than maybe thirty minutes at a time. His dreams were reminiscent of the flashbacks he had had just after serving a combat tour in Iraq. He never pursued the post-traumatic stress syndrome clinics the Veterans Administration offered him when he got out of the army.

Every so often, Johnnie would make his way to the entrance of the mine, only to be turned back by the heat well before he got there.

He had absolutely no idea how long he'd been in the mine shaft; it seemed like forever, but he suspected it was a lot less time than he even conservatively estimated. The supplies in the mine would last for weeks, if needed, so there was no rush to get going. It was the boredom, mixed with the helplessness and the anxiety that got to him. He had to fight thinking the worst about what may have happened to Missy.

Johnnie ventured to the door again and was now able to get to the entrance without being turned back by the heat. The heat compared to the hottest day he could remember in the Gulf, but was finally within human tolerances. When he peered out, the sky was the blackest black he had ever seen. The wind blew constantly; he could hear the sound of water thrashing in the distance. It was either the Allegheny River, Bull Creek, or maybe even both of them. Johnnie decided to stay patient and wait for things to cool down further, as he now suspected they would over time.

Patience is a virtue he kept reminding himself as he stared at the rock walls of the dimly lit mine.

****

The astronauts stared down at an almost unrecognizable planet. The entire surface was now covered with a dark gray cloud. On the night side of earth, the sky lit up brilliantly from time to time from lightning. Dick Ford could still see debris randomly falling to the surface, but there was not as much as before.

The crew had had a scare about a day earlier when a piece of golf ball-sized space debris burst right through one of the modules. The astronauts were able to seal the rupture and later patch the holes. Dick planned a space walk to check for additional damage to the space station once things had stabilized further.

****

President Stockwell looked to his staff for updates—but there were none. Chip said, "They lost contact with NORAD in Cheyenne Mountain a couple hours ago." The only news of the outside world came from several enlisted men and an officer who went out the Site R blast door. They reported that the temperature had dropped to about 100 degrees, with the sky completely blacked out and the wind blowing violently. They noted that all the cars in the parking lot had had their windows shattered, less the front windshields that fared only a little better with the protective shatterproof coating.

On a different subject, another aide said that they had supplies to last over a year and a half for this contingent of survivors at Site R, assuming the Cold War rations hadn't spoiled and the water treatment equipment held.

CHAPTER 11
Day 3: Room Temperature

"It doesn't make a difference what temperature a room is, it's always room temperature."
Steven Wright

The Colonel stepped outside today to absolute darkness. The temperature had dropped to about 75 degrees. A balmy wind blew harder than the day before while the torrential sound of the river below seemed to have dissipated somewhat. The Colonel went back up to the house and looked for additional items such as clothing and other non-edible but useful supplies. Kaitlin joined him in carrying the various supplies back to the cave. They made five trips with the wheelbarrow.

The Colonel tried to start Regis's car, with no success; Kaitlin's Kia Borrego would not crank either; it would not even make the distinctive clicking noise of an almost dead battery. The Colonel's vintage truck in the garage fared better, with the windows cracked but not shattered. The truck however, had no battery, so that was a dead end.

The Colonel told Kaitlin to head back to the cave while he checked on the neighbors. He suspected this would not be a pleasant task. With his 30-30 slung over his shoulder and flashlight in hand, he walked down Sportsman Road to check on the other houses in the area. The same road that had been covered three days ago with over a foot of snow, was now clear. Small branches covered the roadway and most trees were still upright and intact.

The Colonel approached the first neighbor's house, a 1970s split level. He noticed all the windows had been blown out and that there was debris in the yard; he knocked on the door. He then opened the front door and kept yelling, "Anyone there? It's Bob Steele, Ernie, Mary Lou—are you all there?"

He then opened the door and walked around the upstairs, noticing the putrid sweet smell he remembered from his Vietnam days; he then went down into the basement, assuming as most folks would, that they'd gone underground to get away from the heat. No stranger to death, he was still in shock at the sight of his neighbors' corpses huddled together in a corner; they looked like they were cooked alive and now were bloated. Even their German shepherd lay beside them, dead.

The Colonel went to the next neighbor's house and found the same situation. This pattern repeated itself for the next eight houses down his rural road.

Finally, he went to farmer Rock's house and found the young couple who'd inherited the farm house from their grandfather, Steve Rock. The couple was alive, but barely. They had held out in an old root cellar their grandfather made by closing off the vents and doors to block the heat. The root cellar was not as good as the cave—the temperature was over 120 degrees for more than twenty hours, but the young couple had survived the heat's onslaught.

The Colonel got them some water; they were still in shock from all that had happened over the last several days.

The young farmer, Kevin Rock, finally started to come around and asked, "What happened?" when he realized the Colonel was not a hallucination. His wife Jennifer was still in shock. The Colonel tried to explain all he knew regarding the impacts, but it was not much more than Kevin already knew. The couple had a lot of food in the cellar, and a well with a hand pump in the basement that was still operational. After they appeared to be all right, the Colonel told them to sit tight and he'd come back in a few days to check up on them.

****

The VMI cadets finally emerged from the tunnels. The air outside was cool compared to a day earlier, and the sky pitch black. The wind and rain had a bone chilling bite to it as it swirled through the campus buildings. After scoping out the campus and immediate surrounding area, the Gunny Sergeant had all the cadets form up at Cameron Hall near the football field. The Gunny asked Van Price, to assemble his company commanders to discuss their next step.

The Gunny Sergeant told the cadet leaders that he had not found anyone alive above ground when he did a survey of some of the houses around Lexington. The Gunny knew the town of Lexington had minimal supplies for what the cadets would require to survive in the coming months. He suspected, as they all did, that the weather would most likely take a turn for the worse and get very cold, and soon.

The Gunny proposed breaking the corps of cadets up into eight smaller groups by company, with the current leadership in place, and have them disperse in different directions from Lexington to better forage for supplies. He said, "The plan is to meet here, if and when the weather improves, listen for my signal."

"I, along with some of the infirmed cadets, will use the tunnel system as a headquarters." He added, "While we are separated into our various groups, I expect each of the cadets to live up to the honor of our corps by helping all those they come across."

The company commanders all crisply responded, "Yes, Gunny Sergeant."

ANTHONY G. SHEA, JR.

****

Johnnie peeked out of the mine entrance again, and was now finally able to step outside comfortably. The air had a chill to it; the sky was darker than a new-moon night. "Even the stars on such a night would have provided more light than how it was right now," Johnnie said out loud.

Lightning broke the darkness from time to time. Johnnie decided he better get some supplies and try to make it to the Colonel's house before the weather changed. He fashioned a backpack of sorts from the miner survival gear for the trip to the Colonel's cave, packing food, a tarp, a sleeping bag, and some extra clothes.

Johnnie estimated it was about twenty miles to the house as the crow flies, maybe thirty if he had to take the roads versus railroad bridges between Freeport and Schenley. In theory, this walk would take about four to five hours; he had done further hikes in the Army, and he was still in pretty good shape, running half marathons and other races in the area. Johnnie had even kicked around the idea of running the entire Pittsburgh Marathon this coming year.

The road out of the Tour-Ed Mine entrance was strewn with debris. Johnnie walked down to Route 28, then headed north on the northbound lane since it had fewer cars on it than the southbound lane going into Pittsburgh. The southbound lane was littered with cars from the traffic jam that had occurred just prior to the impacts. Johnnie was surprised to look in a couple of the cars and see dead bodies. They looked as though they had been cooked alive. The traffic jam of cars cleared up at about Exit 15, several miles up the road. Jonnie noticed the air seemed to be getting colder, even in the time he had been walking.

He cut up Burtner Road, planning to walk up old Route 28 through Natrona Heights. To his surprise, he had yet to see another living soul, or any light in any of the houses.

The wind howled through the leafless trees, ash from the impact and fires stuck to every surface. About the time Johnnie got to old Route 28, it started to storm violently. The thunder sounded like the artillery attacks he had heard in Iraq. Johnnie made his way to the McDonalds in Natrona Heights. The windows had shattered, but the building still offered some protection from the elements.

Johnnie yelled inside but got no answer. It was spooky; no one seemed to be around. Johnnie went in the back way and opened the walk-in cooler, and to his absolute horror saw many people squeezed in it and all dead. It appeared the cooler had stayed cool for awhile but finally heated up as well. Johnnie collected several additional canned goods from the McDonald's for his trip to the cave.

After the storm had passed, Johnnie pressed on with his journey to the cave. Three more miles up the road, he came to the Super Wal-Mart in Natrona Heights. Most of the windows were broken there, too. When John went inside, he saw that all the roof windows were shattered as well. Surprisingly, all the merchandise was mostly untouched, though rain came in through the holes in the ceiling. The air in the store already had a musty smell to it.

The grocery section actually had a full compliment of food, but the perishables all were ruined from the intense heat; the smell of the rotting food was overwhelming. Johnnie went back to the sporting goods department and traded his miner's pack for a true hiking backpack. Though Johnnie suspected it was not as high quality as something you could buy at, say, a sporting goods store, the backpack was definitely better than the miner's pack he had lugged on his back the last several miles.

Johnnie then found a three-season pack tent, a smaller sleeping bag with a better temperature rating that was water resistant, and a backpack stove and fuel. He took every package of Mountain House dehydrated food he could find. Breaking the gun cabinet window, he took down a .22 rifle and several thousand rounds of ammunition. *Not much stopping power, but having a rifle is better than not if truly needed*, he thought to himself.

Johnnie took all the other weapons and ammo and wrapped them in another tent and hid them in cabinet under a DVD shelf; he also loaded shopping cart after shopping cart of canned goods and wrapped them in tents as well and put them in other bins in the electronics area to protect them from the rain. He stopped by the shoe department and found a pair of insulated work boots and tennis shoes, then went to the clothing area, where he got various items, including thermal underwear, extra socks and underwear, and a heavy jacket.

Johnnie had a suspicion the weather was going to turn really cold in the coming days.

Johnnie set out again on the road towards Freeport. Even this stretch of road had a dead car on it every so often. As he walked down Route 28, Johnnie weathered a driving rain that his rain jacket barely held up against. He walked up the entrance to the Freeport Bridge, and to his surprise, the bridge was gone; it had washed out. The road just abruptly ended.

"I'll be darned," Johnnie said out loud. He could not make out the wild flowing river he heard below by shining his flashlight over the edge of the bridge; the beam of his flashlight vanished in a misty abyss.

The weather now turned nastier, with heavy wind and driving rain and a tinge more cold to it. Lightning lit up the Freeport valley and Johnnie could finally see the remnants of the Freeport Bridge. The entire span across the river appeared to have washed away. The Allegheny River appeared many times larger than it normally did.

All Johnnie could do was backtrack up the hill towards Natrona Heights. When he got to the top of the hill, he headed down the road past the Cherapp Ford dealership for the bypass to Route 28 again in hopes of finding an intact bridge across the Allegheny River in Kittanning.

Tired from almost ten miles carrying a heavy backpack, Johnnie took refuge in a BP gas station next to the Route 28 exit and locked himself into the windowless restroom. He set up his tent by flashlight in the room and slept for over 10 hours straight. Outside, the wind and rain belted out a continual moan.

****

"Mr. President, we've contacted one of our subs in the south Atlantic, they were off the shore of Argentina when the impact occurred," Chip reported to the commander in chief in the Site R communications room. "The commander of the sub asked for orders on how to proceed," he said.

An order like this, to most presidents, might have seemed odd, but to him, being former military, it wasn't. "How are they on fuel?" asked the president.

"They have enough nuclear fuel to last for over five years," Chip replied, anticipating the question.

"How about food?"

"They have about eight month's worth, give or take."

"Have them survey the continents around the world taking note of damage, survivors, and potential habitable land, procuring needed supplies along the way, and have them report back to Site R the first of every month with a situation report," the President ordered, not missing a beat. "What's the sub commander's name?" he asked, as if hoping to know him.

"Captain Glenn Bagley," replied Chip.

The president did not know him. "Thanks, Chip."

The president went back to reading some old report on the effects of nuclear winter from the site's library.

CHAPTER 12
Day 4: Getting Cooler

"The general trend in the last 4,000 years is that carbon dioxide and temperature have been moving against each other."

PIERS CORBYN

The temperature was now down to 45 degrees on the thermometer, as the Colonel exited the cave that morning at about 10 a.m. The sky was pitch-black, rain spat down continually and the wind howled as it blew through the trees and rocks on the hillside near the cave entrance. Lightning broke the darkness with blinding flashes. The Colonel and Kaitlin went back up to the house again.

In the Colonel's garage, with his Coleman lantern hanging on the garage door railing, the Colonel looked over the premier set of tools that his dad and he had built up over the years, and grabbed a wrench from the cabinet. The Colonel had a hunch on the truck situation; he was going to take the battery from my car and put it in his truck. With Kaitlin holding a dying flashlight in the mist and rain, the Colonel got the battery out of our car and put it in his truck. The battery sparked as he tightened the battery cable to the positive terminal.

The Colonel said, "This is the moment of truth," looking at Kaitlin as he turned the key.

The old truck cranked and started on the first try immune from the effects EMP.

"Yes," was all the Colonel could say.

The Colonel rushed to manually get the garage door opened up—not an easy task. Even with the windows blown out, the fumes would still start to build up quickly in the semi-enclosed structure.

"It's amazing how you take things for granted, like garage door openers," Kaitlin said as the Colonel struggled with the door.

The Colonel said, "Hop in," and they backed out of the driveway. For just a moment, Kaitlin thought that things were back to normal. Then the realization of the truth of the situation hit her when she tried to tune in the radio and no stations came in on either the FM or AM bands.

The Colonel had to drive slowly to maneuver around all the debris on the old country roads. They drove past the farm house where the Rocks lived and saw candle light in one of the windows. The couple had used plastic to cover over all the windows in the house. They saw Missy's car just past the farmer's house on the side of the road and other cars that had just stopped like Missy's along the road here and there from the EMP shock wave.

At one point, the Colonel had to drive through someone's yard to get past a fallen tree and almost got stuck in the mud. He got out to the main road and made his way to Leechburg, and neither he nor Kaitlin saw another survivor the entire way into town. In Leechburg, he drove to the municipal building to see if there were any survivors or any available information. No one was to be found anywhere in town.

The Colonel then drove to the local IGA grocery store and found it unoccupied. He walked in through one of the broken windows and saw it still had most of its goods on the shelves. The Colonel suspected the owner just locked the door when the power got knocked out and walked home. Thinking ahead, the Colonel told Kaitlin to start loading up the truck with non-perishable canned goods. The Colonel also loaded up on batteries and cleaning supplies and took all the bird seed in the store for the animals, as well as several bags of dog food for his dog, Molly, now living in the cave with them.

The Colonel and Kaitlin loaded everything that would fit in the truck and headed back to the cave. The wind was blowing and it seemed that even in the time they had been in the store loading supplies the temperature had dropped several degrees. The trip back to the Colonel's house, which would have taken ten minutes before the impacts, now took an hour and a half. The entire family unloaded the truck in the garage, and the Colonel asked Missy to go back to town to get another truck load of supplies.

The way the temperature was dropping concerned the Colonel and he did not want to wait; he'd stop by the young couple's house and offer to have them load up a truck load of supplies as well before the end of the day.

At the house, Kaitlin and Mom wheelbarrowed the loads of goods from the store down to the cave. I took inventory of everything brought into the cave. I knew the Colonel would want a status of supplies when he finished up for the day. Knowing the old man, he'd also want to know how long they could last with the new supplies added into the current supplies, as well as items still needed.

****

Johnnie awoke about 5 a.m. to the sound of the wind blowing something around outside the gas station. It was hard to tell what day it was, let alone discern if it were even day or night. Johnnie estimated that he was now only three miles from the Colonel's house. However, he knew with the Freeport bridge gone, the game had changed. Having not seen a single other living person since just after the impact, Johnnie started wondering if the Colonel, Missy, and family were still alive; he wondered if anyone was alive at this point. Being a social person by nature, Johnnie realized how crazy one can get having no one to talk to for, even for just a couple days.

He used the backpack stove to heat up water to reconstitute a package of dehydrated scrambled eggs and bacon and he drank a lukewarm bottle of soda from the store. Johnnie looked around inside the BP station for any last-minute supplies, taking some beef jerky and a couple of Gatorades. He then set out on foot toward Kittanning. *If the bridge survived over Buffalo Creek up the road on Route 28, possibly the high-span bridge over the Allegheny River between Kittanning and Ford City has, too,* he thought to himself; but he did not have a plan if the bridge was out.

Johnnie stepped outside and looked around. It was completely dark; the visibility was in feet, with a misty rain in the beam of his flashlight. Johnnie saw abandoned cars still at the gas pumps, some with the nozzles still in the gas tanks, their occupants long gone. One of the gas nozzles lay on the ground beside an SUV. The wind howled through the abandoned pumps. With some struggle, Johnnie made it to Route 28. Even though it was a main highway, his being on foot made the journey slow and arduous.

The road had dead cars on it, but at a less frequency as he headed north. After an hour's walk, Johnnie made it to the bridge over Buffalo Creek. It had survived, giving Johnnie hope that the bridge across the Allegheny River might have survived as well.

Johnnie pressed northward. As he trudged along the highway, the wind seemed to get colder and colder by the hour. But what was an hour anymore? His watch did not work and he no way to gauge elapsed time. He didn't even know if it was day or night.

Two more hours of walking got Johnnie just about to the outskirts of West Kittanning. He walked up over the side of the road to the Armstrong County Memorial Hospital. Johnnie was familiar with the hospital and had visited Missy for lunch there from time to time. To his surprise, he saw a light in the hospital by the emergency room entrance. He walked up to the door and hollered, "Hello! Anyone in there?"

Out came four men and a woman. The men looked kind of scary with their soot-covered faces, but they were all decent people once Johnnie got to talking to them. The men said they had been deep underground at the Rosebud Coal Mine over in Slate Lick and the woman was in the mine office when the impacts happened. When they tried to leave, their cars would not start, and all the power was out, less the lighting in the mine itself, which ran on battery backup power.

"Most the miners in the mine that day chose to leave on foot right away, but we all lived too far away in Cranberry Township, and decided to see if the power would come back on; it did not," said the one older miner.

"It then got real hot, and we stayed in the mine the last couple days," another miner said.

"We came here to get medical care for Buddy, who burned his hands trying to check outside when it was still hot," the older miner said. He said the woman who was with them appeared to have bad earaches from the concussion.

Buddy said, "Other than the miners, you are the first survivor besides us we've seen. About eight other miners we were with originally parted ways with us yesterday, heading towards Butler following Route 422."

"We've seen a lot of dead bodies in the hospital's basement; I suppose they were trying to get away from the heat," said the older miner.

"We've found the supplies here I needed to fix my hands," Buddy said as he readjusted the bandage on his hand.

The woman said, "There is a lot of food here, too, so we are planning to stay for a little while. Do you know what happened?"

Her name was Rita and she talked loudly because her ears were ringing.

Johnnie said, "I heard on the radio there was possibly an asteroid or comet on a collision course with the earth. The power went out shortly after that, even my car would not start." He spoke loudly and looked straight at Rita so she could hear and understand him.

"I was down on Route 28 near Tarentum, stuck in a traffic jam, when it all went down," he said to the group. "All the cars went dead; I suspect it was some type of EMP from the impact. About half the folks stayed with their cars and the other half headed into Tarentum," he said. "I tried talking folks into joining me at the Tour-Ed Mine but no one came; seems like you all survived the same way. Now I am trying to get to Leechburg to see my family. I need to find a way to get across the Allegheny River—the bridge in Freeport was out."

Johnnie went on. "I also have a feeling it is going to get real cold for awhile, like some sort of nuclear winter, and I recommend you all find a place to hunker down for awhile yourselves."

He decided to stay at the hospital to sleep for awhile and then head out again after he was rested. Truthfully, Johnnie wanted to be around other people, at least for a little while. With supplies seemingly numerous for the few folks left alive, Johnnie somehow suspected companionship was what people would now crave. By the time everyone finally went to sleep, Johnnie knew the life story of each person in the group. Johnnie suspected all the families and friends of the group at the hospital were gone; he still had his doubts that his own wife, Missy, was still alive. But he had some hope now, seeing some other survivors. *If anyone could pull it off, it would be the Colonel.* Johnnie kept holding out that thought.

CHAPTER 13
Day 5: Below Freezing

"We could face cold conditions, but you never know what the weather will bring there."
RALF SCHUMACHER

The Colonel tasked me to come up with a list of needed supplies, taking into account all that was brought to the cave yesterday from town. I asked him, somewhat rhetorically, "How long do I plan for, Colonel?"

He replied, "For at least two years, and most likely much longer."

I came up with a long list of supplies that ranged from food to medical supplies to vitamins and toiletries to toilet paper, hardware, and even diapers, plus bottles and formula, and much more dog food. I also added grain for the animals and any seeds that could be found, just in case the weather cooperated again at some point in the future. I wished I had bought those non-hybrid seeds I heard advertised on the Glenn Beck show.

Missy said she would go into town with the Colonel to gather medical supplies, given her background in the medical field. The Colonel exited the cave door and could tell it was noticeably colder now than yesterday. The sky was still pitch-black, with the wind howling its continuous song through the rocks and trees. The Colonel did not even check the thermometer today when he left; he estimated the temperature was now in the mid-thirties, though, and it was still spitting rain. The Colonel knew the outing would do Missy good and get her mind off Johnnie.

The Colonel drove down the road to the Rocks' house and told them they were going back into to town to scavenge for more supplies, and to make a list; the Colonel said he would come back in about two or three hours to take them to town for another run, too.

The Colonel had learned the ins and outs of the debris-covered post-impact roads, and was now able to get to town in about thirty minutes. The first stop this day was the Klingensmith Drugstore. The Colonel kicked in the shattered glass on the door, and he and Missy walked into the drugstore. Missy went back to the bulk prescription area and loaded up three large garbage bags with various containers of all sorts of prescription drugs she thought might be useful. The Colonel started loading cans of Ensure and the little bit of canned food that was in the drugstore.

Though not really a smoker, the Colonel loaded up on all the cigars the store had; he enjoyed smoking a good stogie every once in a while. The Colonel also made a mental note to see if there was anything salvageable at the Wine and Spirits store if time and the weather both allowed. The Colonel and Missy then went to the grocery store in Leechburg and loaded the truck again, which was overflowing with supplies. It appeared that no one had grabbed so much as a candy bar since the Colonel was there yesterday. The town, as far as he could tell, was a complete ghost town; he did not see anyone or any bodies in the stores or in the streets. He stopped at the Wine and Spirits store and loaded the cab with hooch until there was only enough room for Missy and him to sit down.

After everyone unloaded the truck, the Colonel drove to the Rocks' and picked them up for another run into town. The Colonel asked if the farmer's wife, Jennifer, would want to go to the cave while he and Kevin went to town. Jennifer said yes, she looked forward to talking to other women. The sheer boredom of being in their house twenty-four hours a day was driving her nuts.

****

"President Stockwell, we've made contact today with the International Space Station," Chip said, entering the president's study. "They say they are doing fine and have enough supplies plus oxygen to last almost two years, if need be."

"What did they see?" President Stockwell asked.

"Dick Ford said they saw two asteroids hit the earth and that the one in the Pacific created a firestorm that burned most of the way across the United States to about eastern Ohio before it finally dissipated. The second asteroid hit just west of Europe, enveloping most of Europe in the ensuing firestorm."

Chip continued, "Dick Ford further told me that the entire globe is now covered in a thick ash cloud, with no apparent sunlight making it to surface, as best he could tell. Their scientist believes temperatures across the globe will drop well below freezing for over a year, until the atmospheric dust cloud dissipates."

"Jesus," was all the president could mumble.

"As far as survivors in the US, the best we can theorize is only people from about middle Ohio and east to the Appalachian Mountain chain had a shot, and only if they could get underground during the forty hours the temperature rose above 350 degrees," Chip explained. "Everyone on the eastern seaboard most likely died from tsunamis created from the European impact; our on-site meteorologist believes the firestorm from the Pacific strike was stopped short of engulfing the entire United States only because of the massive cold front hovering over the Eastern US," Chip said as a consolation. "Otherwise, the entire North American continent would have been completely sterilized of life. As it is, we estimate less than 15,000 people are still alive in the continental United States, half those being military that had access to adequate shelter."

Chip did not even discuss Alaska and Hawaii.

The President was speechless after hearing Chip's report.

"We estimate the world population is now less than 200,000, with a lot of those surviving being Swiss. The Swiss had planned for World War III and had a complex system of shelters in their country; the question is how many of their citizens got to the shelters in the confusion."

"Most of the shelters are in the Swiss Alps and the population is in the cities," Chip explained.

****

Johnnie set out from the Armstrong County Memorial Hospital to find a means to cross the Allegheny River. The walk from the hospital to the bridge was only a couple more miles, at best. But it took him five hours; with no light, he was disoriented and ended up walking the wrong direction toward West Kittanning before catching on and then having to circle back.

The moment of truth came as Johnnie walked down the four-lane highway to the Route 422 bridge across the Allegheny River. Johnnie stepped out onto the bridge ever so cautiously. He could hear the water raging below, but could not actually see down to it over the bridge's side; his flashlight was unable to penetrate the heavy mist and spitting rain to the river below. Johnnie could not see the distant end of the bridge, either. Step by step through the darkness, he made his way carefully across the bridge. The bridge had held!

Once across, Johnnie set up camp under the approach bridge to get out of the elements and get some rest; he was not tired so much from physical exertion, but from the stress of it all. His tent was difficult to set up in the darkness and ever-blowing wind. But Johnnie made do, finally drifting off to sleep.

****

The Colonel and Kevin unloaded all the canned goods into the farmer's house; they used a spare bedroom to store the food. The Colonel could have sworn he saw snowflakes, and not rain now, in the truck's headlights. He and the farmer then spent the next three hours packing the farmer's garage with even more firewood for the farmer's wood stove; they pushed out one of the cars to make room for the firewood. Kevin's Power Wagon sat dead in the yard.

Kevin told the Colonel that he had even more wood out in the yard that he could stack in the garage and basement over the next day or two, and that what he had was already more than enough for the winter.

The Colonel said, "Let's get you loaded for the next year as well; it may be even longer than either you or I suspect before it eventually warms up."

Without further talk, both men took load after load of firewood into the garage and tightly packed it in.

"What are you doing for water again?" the Colonel asked.

"We have a hand-pumped well in the basement, and it appears to be working good," Kevin said.

They finally drove back to the cave, exhausted from their work. The women had been worried about them being gone for so long. The Colonel told the Rocks that they were welcome to come and visit anytime; then he and Missy drove them back to their house.

CHAPTER 14
Day 6: The Coming Storm

"The wise man in the storm prays to God, not for safety from danger, but deliverance from fear."
RALPH WALDO EMERSON

"Working many hours straight, I have compiled a rough inventory of all the supplies on hand so far," I reported to the group, whose candle-lit faces huddled around the card table.

"It is absolutely impossible to plan for every contingency," I said. However, I had made a plan for the Colonel, just as he'd requested. "We have enough food and toiletries, if used sparingly, to last two years from all your trips to the supermarket," I said. The Colonel, I knew, was a stickler for trying to carve order out of the chaos.

"However, I made a list of additional supplies."

The Colonel had opened the door that day to find the weather was now between sleeting and snowing. The air had an absolute bone-chilling feel to it. The Colonel, Missy, and Kaitlin all went to town this time. The Colonel stopped at the farmer's house and told them to make a list of things they had missed and he'd stop by later to take them for another run into town. In the last two days, Kevin had filled his garage, basement, and spare rooms with firewood. The Colonel's truck slid now, as he drove into town on the sleeted roads; the truck's headlights cut through the snow and sleet in the absolute darkness. The road was trackless except for the Colonel's truck's tire prints

In town, the Colonel and the girls once again loaded the truck with supplies. The town was absolute pitch black. Kaitlin said, "Let's stop by the bookstore, Beans and Books, to load up on reading material." Her suspicion was they would be cooped up for awhile with the weather turning cold again; reading material would help fight the extreme boredom of being holed up in the cave. The Colonel and the girls ran four loads of supplies, versus the three they had planned, hitting the Dollar General store for additional canned goods. Exhausted, the Colonel kept his word and stopped back at Rocks' to take them for one more supply run. This time the Colonel took Jennifer along, too.

****

Johnnie woke up under the bridge the next day to his hand falling asleep. Johnnie had laid his head on it for a pillow; he was now shaking it, trying to get the pins and needles sensation to go away. The weather was much colder and the rain had turned to sleet and snow. Johnnie ate a breakfast of dehydrated Mountain House beef stew, and then packed up camp. The supplies Johnnie had in his pack were still plentiful, with at least five more days' worth, though he felt grungy from no shower in almost a week. With backpack and rifle on his back, Johnnie set out on Route 66 south for Leechburg.

The road was slick, and hard to walk on, with a snow and sleet combination sticking to it. Looking down over the hill into Ford City, Johnnie saw the flickering light of a town-wide fire. The noxious fumes blew in his direction with a shift of the wind, and made him nauseous.

Johnnie came upon a Sheetz convenience store along Route 66 on the hill above Ford City. It looked like someone had been inside; the shelves were emptied of goods. However, Johnnie was still able to grab two bottles of soda from the now defunct cooler. Johnnie also grabbed numerous power and candy bars that had not melted in the heat wave.

As Johnnie stepped out of the store, he saw an older couple walking up towards him; the man was holding a rifle, not quite aimed at him.

All Johnnie could say was "Hi."

The woman yelled at the man—most likely her husband—"Calm down, Bill, lower your rifle." She asked Johnnie in a friendly voice, "Where are you heading?"

Johnnie replied, grateful of her coolness, "to Leechburg to try to find my family, ma'am."

The woman said that she and her husband had survived by going into their old Cold War bomb shelter. "You are the first human we have seen since it has cooled," she said.

Johnnie explained how he took shelter in the Tour-Ed Mine. Johnnie's easygoing personality finally calmed the man down, though he charmed the older woman with just his smile.

The couple told him that they also had two grandchildren in tow; they had been babysitting when the power went out and they doubted they would ever see their daughter or son-in-law again. They had been on their way to Pittsburgh for work when the asteroids hit. Johnnie recollected the traffic jam on Route 28 the day of the impacts.

"Do you all have the supplies you need to get yourselves through the winter?" he asked them. The man said, "Yes," but there was a lingering distrustful look in his eyes.

Johnnie asked what they were doing for heat and water. The man, a Korea and Vietnam veteran, appeared to have everything under control, saying he had enough wood for his wood burner to last over a year and that he melted snow and boiled it for water. Though melting snow was time-consuming, all anyone had any more was time.

Johnnie asked, "Is there anything I can do to help you all out?"

The man politely declined.

Johnnie headed down Route 66 toward Leechburg. The road was strewn with debris that had washed out from creeks running along the side of the roadway, plus there were several cars every so often along the way. Johnnie walked about four miles, he estimated, to about where Garda's Italian Restaurant was, close to where Crooked Creek crosses the road, where he set up camp for the evening. Johnnie's intuition led him to believe the road would be washed out, but he did not want to deal with that until tomorrow morning—though Johnnie could not really tell night from day anymore.

Just before getting camp set up, Johnnie went into Garda's Restaurant looking for survivors; but none were to be found alive. It was the same story, with folks in the basement who had died from the heat. Johnnie then went to the restaurant's cabinets and replenished his food supplies for his pack; he was also able to scrounge several sodas and even a couple cans of beer. Johnnie then set his tent up inside a fire department training building for shelter from the elements. Almost immune from the carnage of the dead bodies he saw at the restaurant, it didn't take long until Johnnie was asleep.

CHAPTER 15
1 Week: Normalcy

"The only normal people are the ones you don't know very well."
JOE ANCIS

Normalcy—how does one define it anymore? I thought to myself this morning as I wrote my journal entry. I've never really known normalcy like most folks, being handicapped all my life.

It has been a week since the impacts. I have been busier than I have ever been in my life, going over inventories of food and supplies; so much hinged on calculating everything right down to the last can of beans.

Normalcy is maybe the wrong word to use; routine may be a better one. Dad, or the Colonel—I even called him that before impact—had his daily meeting of the family that day in the cabin's map room, where I reported our current status.

"According to my calculations, we now have over three years worth of supplies with yesterday's truck loads of supplies," I told the group. ", from salt and spices, to clothing and shoes, to additional toiletries and various medical books that may be useful if you all can get out today." I handed the updated list to the Colonel.

I had even suggested looking at the churches in town for votive candles in glass holders, for additional light. Candles not in glass containers had melted into unrecognizable masses of wax during the heat wave.

"As long as trips can be made to town, we need to keep stocking up on any and all supplies," I said, all agreed.

With the weather getting colder and snowier, and with the perpetual darkness, the suspicion was that it would not be long until the roads were impassable, and we'd be cave-bound for a while.

The Colonel found several walkie-talkies that Pap had packed away in the supply room years ago. "They appear to work at close range, possibly a mile or two," the Colonel said. I said, "My thoughts are that we give one to Rocks and work out a plan to communicate with them if the weather worsens."

"My thoughts exactly, Regis," the Colonel concurred. "They should reach the farmer's house if we stand at the cave entrance, and the farmers on the side of their house facing the cave."

The Colonel also found an old ham radio and antenna he wanted to set up, weather permitting. Pap also had an old World War II hand-cranked battery charger with batteries ready to set up the system. With the Colonel's knowledge of military radio communications, he may have been able to contact someone if they had a comparable set. We fashioned an outlet with a fluorescent light plugged into it using a car battery and a DC inverter. The bright light was appreciated by all, but we all knew it would not last forever.

The Colonel and Kaitlin set out for the day's supply run. The Colonel barely got up the hill in four-wheel drive; they both knew this would probably be the last day they'd get out to town. The snow was about eight inches now and flurrying with intermittent squalls through the beams of their headlights.

"There will be no one to clear the roads, so the snow will keep piling up," Kaitlin said as the Colonel spun his wheels to get up over the hill on the Old Schenley Road.

The Colonel dropped off a walkie-talkie and several dozen nine-volt batteries to the Rocks and said they'd set up a schedule to talk. For now, the Colonel told Kevin, the plan was to talk at noon to check in on each other for about five minutes only, to conserve the batteries.

Kaitlin and the Colonel loaded up the truck once again with supplies from the Save a Lot and Kmart from Allegheny Township. The Colonel found several cases of nine-volt batteries and even picked up two dozen additional car batteries just in case from a garage at the top of the hill near Leechburg. On the way out of town, Kaitlin said, "Let's stop at the Krutz Jewelry Shop."

Miffed, the Colonel did so.

Kaitlin said, "Let's get as many wind-up watches and clocks as we can, otherwise, we will not be able to line up times with the Rocks to talk on the walkie talkies."

"Good idea," the Colonel said, understanding the gist of her thought now. "Also, let's look for old-fashioned battery clocks, they may still work," the Colonel suggested.

On the way back, the Colonel gave the Rocks three watches, two clocks synchronized with the watches, and another case of nine-volt batteries and took Kevin to town for a supply run while Kaitlin talked to Jennifer by wood burner stove in the living room. Jennifer poured Kaitlin a cup of tea. "Do you think it will ever get better again" Kaitlin asked. Kaitlin's facial expressions betrayed her words when she said "yes." The conversation then changed to Kaitlin's due date and the conversation lightened.

By the time the Colonel and Kaitlin pulled in the driveway from their last load of the day, the snowstorm was almost a blizzard, with snow blowing in the beams of the flashlights. Visibility was in feet; the temperature was now in the teens.

The Colonel picked up Kevin for his last load of supplies. After the Rock's unloaded their supplies, the Colonel drove home and parked his truck in the garage, disconnected the battery, and filled the oil up to the opening on the truck's valve cover. The Colonel then covered the truck with a large plastic tarp, holding the tarp down to the garage floor with a series of logs.

The Colonel found a can of red spray paint and left a message on the wall inside the garage: *Johnnie we are alive—stick to the plan. Bob.* The Colonel knew Johnnie would be smart enough to find the cave if he saw the message. The Colonel then trudged over the hillside down to the cave entrance through the ever deepening snow. He closed the cave door to the blizzard outside and locked it; the temperature outside was now 15 degrees.

Inside the cave, it was a lukewarm 52 degrees and smelled like a barn. The Colonel checked on the animals; they were doing as well as could be expected under the circumstances. In fact, some of the chickens had laid some eggs. The cave was big, but they would have to work a plan before long for manure disposal.

With the weather turning worse, and a week having passed, Missy realized that Johnnie was probably not still alive. The group realized they would now need to hunker down in the cave for the long run. All knew it might be a while before the weather improved again and daylight returned.

CHAPTER 16
The Blizzard

"The blizzard of the world has crossed the threshold and it's overturned the order of the soul."
LEONARD COHEN

Johnnie awoke to the wind violently blowing his tent as the snow built up on it on the leeward side. Eight days since the impact, and the weather was the worst he had ever seen in his entire life. He ate a breakfast of several canned goods from the restaurant, drank several pops; he had found that keeping them in his sleeping bag had kept them from freezing.

Without delay, Johnnie set out for the day, but he did not get even a mile down the road before he saw that the road was washed out and was a large span of water. The newly formed flow was fifty feet wide going through what once was Route 66. Crooked Creek had apparently filled up and was now going through the emergency spillway, diverted from its normal channel; the new flow had cut right through the road in the process. The farthest Crooked Creek had ever gone before the impacts was ten feet down from the emergency spillway during the storms spun off by Hurricane Agnes back in 1972.

Johnnie pondered how to get to the other side through the raging torrent of dark, muddy water with large pieces of ice piled up on both shores. One slip and he'd be dead. He suspected the few small downstream bridges between Crooked Creek were most likely washed out as well. Upstream was Crook Creek Lake, with maybe thirty to forty miles needed to traverse it the long way around; this did not appear to him to be a viable option. Most likely, the feeder streams to the lake had had their bridges washed out as well.

Less than twenty miles from home, and I might as well have be a thousand or a million, Johnnie thought. *I am no better off now than when I was on stalled out on Route 28 near Tarentum.*

Johnnie backtracked up Route 66 and looked for the road to the lake, but scratched that thought as the weather worsened. Besides the darkness, the visibility was limited from the blowing snow. The weather was downright cold and deteriorating by the hour. Johnnie realized he could not travel much longer in this type of weather and headed back to Ford Cliff to find shelter. He made it back to Ford Cliff and camped out in the windowless IGA.

Johnnie fell asleep, exhausted from all the walking, but he was never really in a deep sleep for all that long.

****

When the Colonel opened the cave door the next day, he almost got blown over by the wind. It was an absolute blizzard outside.

By now the roads must have become impassible, he thought.

The Colonel was glad he had parked the truck in the garage, putting the tires on wood and taking out the battery. Standing by the cave door, the Colonel called the Rocks on the walkie-talkies.

"We are doing well, Colonel," Kevin reported, but secretly he and Jennifer were fighting boredom from being cooped up in the farmhouse. "We're keeping the house warm with the wood burner."

The Colonel warned, "Be very careful when cleaning out the cinders from the fireplace, have lots of water on hand."

From the food the Rock's had in the root cellar, plus the food the Colonel helped them get from the abandoned supermarket in Leechburg, they were stocked for well over two years, if push really came to shove.

Kevin said, "I wish had gotten more dog food for our puppy, Max."

****

Chip told the president that General Hawk had stepped out of the Cheyenne Mountain complex for the first time since the day of the impacts to get a visual of the damage. He had reported that "every last stick was burned away in Colorado Springs" from the firestorm. "The weather seemed more like Antarctica than Colorado, he said.

He added that they had contact established now with another secret military base in Montana, several of the missile silo control bunkers, but doubted the actual missiles would even fire anymore. Touching on national security, the general said, "The only known nuclear capability of the United States that was left was one nuclear submarine."

The president and personnel at Site R had already talked to the sub captain earlier.

CHAPTER 17
Refuge

> *"My house is my refuge, an emotional piece of architecture, not a cold piece of convenience."*
> LUIS BARRAGAN

After backtracking to Ford Cliff, Johnnie found a house with a wood burner and a lot of firewood stacked up around it. It was close to a mom and pop IGA grocery store. Johnnie had to remove the bodies from the basement that were in the home. And with the ground now frozen, Johnnie moved the bodies to the backyard, covered them with plastic and then snow and said a prayer, making the sign of the cross as he finished.

Johnnie got the fireplace going in short order; the wood stove heated the entire downstairs. Thinking ahead, Johnnie put large pots of snow on top of the wood burner to melt for water. He then made trip after trip to the adjacent grocery store, getting every supply he could imagine. He kept this up for almost ten hours straight, keeping the fire going in between trips. Johnnie kept at it for the next week, fighting through the blizzard, until the house was full of supplies, as well as firewood. The temperature outside was now below zero, and the sky was still pitch black.

The world has gone crazy, Johnnie thought.

Johnnie's only solace now was his blazing fire, with a sleeping bag on a futon in the living room next to the fireplace of his new-found home.

****

The Colonel spent the next several weeks trying to get an antique ham radio working. He found it in a cabinet in the cabin, another legacy of his dad. The Colonel and I read all the radio's manuals to ensure we set it up correctly. The set-up required an outside antenna and power from a series of twelve-volt car batteries. We used the hand crank generator to recharge each of the car batteries individually. I worked with the Colonel to rig up the hand charger to the various batteries. We decided it would be safer to only charge the batteries with the ham radio disconnected. Finally, after fiddling with the wires, the lights came on the old tube set, and there was static. The antenna was set up on the rocks outside the cave door.

The Colonel must have systematically gone through every station with no luck; he tried for hours on end making transmissions at the various frequencies. I recharged the extra batteries, changing them out between series of tries. Our combined efforts netted me sore arms and the Colonel a hoarse voice.

Being stuck in the cave now day and night, with the weather outside horrible, the Colonel and I spent days going through the radio frequencies. *Are we at the cave, and the farmers down the road, the only humans left alive in the entire world?* I often wondered to myself during those days.

As the days turned to weeks, we had just about given up any hope of making radio contact when the Colonel passed by a military station and heard a distant voice. The Colonel called out, "This is Colonel retired Robert Steele from Leechburg, Pennsylvania, is there anyone out there—over?"

Just then one of the batteries died. We did not have any recharged batteries ready. "Damn it," was all the Colonel could say. He noted the frequency on the manual dial for when we had the batteries re-charged again.

****

At his acquired home in Ford Cliff, Johnnie had settled into a routine. He kept the fire going perpetually, cleaning out the cinders from under the grate every four or five days. He kept buckets of water on hand lest a cinder fall on the carpet and start a fire.

Johnnie barely left the house now except to make infrequent runs to the store or to bring in more firewood from the garage, and he only did this if the weather seemed to let up some. Johnnie saw tracks at the store one time and suspected they were from the couple he had met at the Sheetz convenience. Johnnie left a note conspicuously inside the store, with the directions to his house across the road, taped to the store's doorway.

Johnnie had begun reading the collection of Civil War books the former owner had in the house. Johnnie used the candles from the Yankee Candle collection from the mom and pop store for light to read by on those perpetually dark days. The wind howled just outside the plastic covered windows, and even with the fire blazing the air in the house always seemed to have a chill on it.

For Johnnie, the boredom of no one to talk to, no television, no music, and a small living room were harder to endure than anything else. He had not quite consigned himself to painting a face on a ball and calling it "Wilson" like the character did in the Tom Hanks movie *Cast Away*, but he was getting close. The boredom was matched by the pure adrenaline needed to go out in the cold to get a missing supply from the store or firewood from the garage, hoping not to get lost in the blowing snow and darkness.

****

"Mr. President, we heard someone on a ham radio earlier," Chip reported as the president looked up from a report he was reading. "The signal was very faint, sir," Chip said, deliberately giving not enough info to spark the president's interest. "The person on the line claimed to be a retired colonel," Chip said.

The president was now fully engaged with the conversation. "What was the name of the colonel?" he asked.

"He said his name was Robert Steele," Chip replied. But he was not quite sure of this information, as he had gotten it at second hand.

The president smiled for the first time since before the day of the impacts. "I'll be damned, that old war horse made it through," he said with a half smirk on his face.

"You know him, sir?"

"I do. When I was governor of Pennsylvania, Colonel Steele worked on my adjutant general's staff," the president said, life coming back into his body. "Bob Steele was also one of my first supporters when I made my bid for president. Were you able to sustain contact with him?"

"No, sir, as quick as the signal came in, it died back out." Chip knew this was not a good answer to give to the president.

"Do what you can to re-establish contact soonest!" ordered the President.

CHAPTER 18
Contact: Week 4

"Each contact with a human being is so rare, so precious, one should preserve it."

ANAIS NIN

With batteries charged and the radio's antenna extended to the top of the hill, the Colonel tried again to reach whomever he had briefly contacted several hours earlier. The Colonel had tried at the radio all day with no success; he did not hear any other voices this time, just static. About to give up, the Colonel followed the cable outside to the antenna and realized the connection had somehow come undone. He fixed the connection and went back in and turned on the radio; he immediately heard voices through the static.

"This is Captain Jim Colvin of the 305th Signal Brigade, is anyone monitoring this frequency?—over"

The Colonel almost jumped out of his seat as he said, "This is Colonel retired Robert Steele of Leechburg, Pennsylvania. What is your location?—over."

"Site R, sir," the captain replied enthusiastically.

The Colonel knew exactly where Site R was; he had been there on more than several occasions with the Pennsylvania adjutant general and governor for various military exercises.

The President grabbed the microphone and asked, "How are you doing, Bob?"

"Good, Mr. President, it is so good to hear from you," said the Colonel, recognizing his voice at once.

The president motioned for everyone to leave the room; all did but a lone Secret Service man, standing out of earshot.

"Bob, who all is with you?"

"My wife, son, daughter-in-law, and her sister. We're in an old Indian cave," the Colonel replied.

"Any word of other survivors that you know of?" asked President Stockwell with some caution in his voice.

"A couple who stayed in an old root cellar down the road made it," reported the Colonel. "The rest of the neighbors in the area are gone; it appears they all were roasted alive in the heat wave of the first days after impact."

"Jesus," said the president, taking in the bad news.

"What happened, Mr. President?" asked the Colonel, wanting the entire story.

"Call me Jim, we go way back," President Stockwell asked.

"You know I can't do that, Mr. President," replied the Colonel.

President Stockwell started to explain, "Bob as you probably heard, we were hit by two asteroids; they came out of nowhere without any warning. I'm now at Site R with family and a skeleton crew of staff. Survivors seem rare, we have been able to contact a few military bases where folks made it to their respective bunkers." The president explained further, "There is only a ribbon of land from the Appalachian Mountains chain to western Ohio that was not outright destroyed by the firestorm, just after the impact; the cold front was just enough to stop the fire storm from the Pacific strike from rolling over all of North America. Everything east of the Appalachians was destroyed by a giant tsunami from the impact on Europe."

The Colonel listened intently to the president.

"Even in this small ribbon of land, to survive you had to be underground in a bunker, mine, or cave, as in your, case and not just in a basement to survive the heat wave. How are your living conditions there, Bob?"

"We have supplies to last over three years in the cave," the Colonel said. "We're pretty much snowed in for now; I suspect most electronics were affected by some type of EMP effect from the impacts themselves. All the cars died, except for the old ones with non-electronic ignitions. The ham radio I am talking on works off of vacuum tubes."

"I believe you are right, Bob, regarding the EMP pulse.

You all hang in there and take care, Bob."

"You too, Mr. President—over," echoed the Colonel.

"Talk to tomorrow—over."

CHAPTER 19
Maternity

"Birth is the sudden opening of a window, through which you look out upon a stupendous prospect. For what has happened? A miracle. You have exchanged nothing for the possibility of everything."

WILLIAM MACNEILE DIXON

The Colonel and the president talked almost daily for the last two months since initially making contact. Their conversations ranged from recalling the old days in the military to daily activities at Site R and the cave to the weather. Neither discussed the future beyond the next time they'd talk again. The weather had not improved, temperature-wise, though the snow accumulation seemed to stop at about four to five feet, with only flurries coming down now, and lots of blowing snow. It was believed it stopped snowing because it was just too cold to do so.

Kaitlin woke me up at about 3 a.m. on June 2, 2012, and matter-of-factly said, "It is time" as we lay scrunched together on the little double bed in the cabin in the cave.

All I could do was to get Missy and Mom. During the last several months, Missy, Kaitlin, and Mom had read up extensively on natural childbirth techniques and planned for this day. Like it had been done a thousand times before, they prepared for the delivery of the baby.

Missy said, "There is still some time yet."

I was anything but calm, cool, or collected and was ordered out of the room by Missy until I could calm down. After a few minutes, I calmed down and came back in and held Kaitlin's hand. The minutes turned to hours, as Kaitlin's body readied itself to have the baby.

Missy said to Kaitlin, "It's time for you to have the baby, honey."

At 2 p.m., without any pain medicine and no complications, thank God, my wife blessed me with a son. It was the first time since the impact that something actually made sense to me. We named him Robert Regis Steele. Kaitlin just cried and smiled at the same time as she held the baby to her breast. It would not be long now until Missy had her baby as well.

The Colonel brought out two cigars and Dad and I celebrated with a good stogie in one of those banner father–son type moments. All three women yelled at Dad and me to go to the other side of the cave. They wanted to keep the smoke away from the baby.

****

"Colonel Steele to Site R—over," said the Colonel, as the radio crackled to life.

"This is Site R—over," the signal officer responded about thirty seconds later.

"Just doing a status check, we have one more person at the cave," the Colonel proudly said.

The president took the microphone and congratulated the Colonel and the entire Steele family. "With all that's gone wrong in the world, it's good to finally hear some good news," the president, said sounding more like a father figure than the president. "How's the weather in western Pennsylvania, Bob?" inquired the President; this was a common topic of conversation.

"Cold, dark, and blowing snow, same as all the other reports," said the Colonel, still exuberant about the birth of his grandson.

Just then the signal officer told the president that the International Space Station was trying to radio in a situation report; the message was urgent.

"Sorry, Bob, will get back with you tomorrow at the same time," the president said, going on to say, "again, congratulations to you and your family for the new little one."

****

"Mr. President, this is Dick Ford of the International Space Station, we saw what appeared to be meteors falling on the earth, sir" said the astronaut with a slight concern in his voice.

"Say again?" said the president.

"It looked like three distinct meteor showers fell upon the earth in the last hour," another astronaut reported on the radio.

Dick took the mike again and elaborated. "The best we could tell, if our instrumentation is working correctly, there was one meteor shower over the United States in the Iowa area, one over the middle of Russia, and one somewhere in the middle of South Africa; all three locations seemed have approximately 250 or so of these meteors rain down on them."

"Do you have any more info on these meteor showers?" inquired the President.

"Negative, Mr. President."

"Any opinions?" asked the president.

"No, Mr. President, but it its highly unlikely, from a statistical standpoint, that three locations would have meteor showers at the same time in such a manner. These meteors seemed to fall almost deliberately in perfect timing with each other, and they are a lot smaller than the asteroids, about the size of a bus each, just guestimating," said Dick.

"How are you and your crew all holding up out there, Dick?" the president asked to change the subject and ease the pressure a little on the crew.

"So far, so good, Mr. President; I keep looking down on the earth hoping to see a break in the dark clouds shrouding the entire planet," Dick said, looking out of the portal window as he spoke.

"Keep us advised of any more updates—over," the president said.

"Yes, Mr. President, we will keep our eyes peeled—over."

****

Johnnie woke up to the sound of pounding on the door and almost jumped out of his sleeping bag at the noise. It was the old man he'd met earlier at the Sheetz store just after the heat wave had ended. Johnnie invited him in.

The man said his name was Bill. His wife's name was Mary, and they were living with their two grandchildren.

Before Johnnie even asked, as if reading his mind, Bill said, "We are holding out fine at the house. Our windows are mainly intact on the house since I opened them before going to the bomb shelter the day of the impacts. They are only cracked versus being shattered, like most windows in the neighborhood," Bill proudly said, making conversation. He said he had since put clear tape over the few cracks to keep them from getting worse.

Johnnie made some hot chocolate for them. To the surprise of both of them, they lived only about a quarter of a mile at best from each other's house's in Ford Cliff.

"I saw the note you left at the store," Bill said. He had the note in his hand. After about fifteen minutes, the two men talked as though they had known each other their entire lives. Johnnie had the most infectious personality, and Bill was a character in his own right.

After about two hours of conversation, Bill said, "I'd better head back, so the missus does not go outside and start looking for me." He gave Johnnie directions to his house and invited him over, then took his leave.

****

In the month following the mysterious "meteor showers," the president asked for updates regarding more of them, but there were none to be had. The president and the Colonel still talked daily, exchanging weather statistics, talk about the baby, and sometimes old war stories. The weather was about the same. The snow had stopped falling but, the wind was still blowing relentlessly.

****

It was on a Tuesday, about 1 p.m., that Missy's water broke. Kaitlin and Mom delivered Missy's baby. Surprisingly, her birth was even easier than Kaitlin's. The birth was bittersweet, Missy cried, because she wished Johnnie were there to see their new baby girl. She named her Anna Marie, after Johnnie's mother.

There was not too much time for Missy to weep. She had to take care of a newborn. The population at the cave had gone from four to six in a month. The Colonel passed on his latest situation report about Missy's new arrival to the president, who once again expressed his sincerest congratulations to the family.

****

On that same Tuesday, Johnnie woke up abruptly with the strangest feeling; he could not explain it. The wind had died down, so he decided to visit Bill, Mary, and their grandkids. After talking to Bill and Mary, Johnnie got down on the floor and played with the two grandchildren. They played blocks and "horsey." It just hit him, bringing him back to reality, sitting on the floor: his child would have been born any day now.

Johnnie then talked to Bill and Mary some more and they celebrated their fellowship with a can of fried Spam, macaroni and cheese, brownies, and Pepsi. Johnnie was thoroughly full and tired; he said he'd come back and visit them soon.

When Johnnie got back to his house, tired as he could be, he still had to get the fire going again from the remaining embers lest he freeze to death while he was sleeping.

He slept afterwards for the longest time since the impacts and awoke to a cold house with only a few embers still smoldering in the wood burner from what had been a fully stacked wood stove when he went to sleep.

CHAPTER 20
Light!

"In the beginning God created the heaven and the earth. And the earth was without form, and void; and darkness was upon the face of the deep. And the Spirit of God moved upon the face of the waters. And God said, Let there be light: and there was light."
GENESIS, 1. 1

By now, eleven months later, everything was routine. The daily check of the weather, the feeding of the animals, the charging of the batteries, the same food, more or less, and daily radio contact with Site R and the Rocks down the road. The only possible excitement was that Jennifer, the farmer's wife, was about two weeks late, and possibly pregnant. "Too much free time, and not too much to do at the farmstead", I thought.

The Colonel came running up to the little cabin in the cave; he was usually the most cool, collected person I've ever known. He yelled out across the cavern, "Regis, you need to come outside for a minute and see this."

I obliged him, getting on my crutches and making my way to the cave door.

"What's different?" the Colonel asked.

The wind had settled down from its usual wild bluster, but was still blowing more than a normal pre-impact day, and the air was a little warmer.

Then it hit me. "The sky looks lighter," I said as I looked skyward.

The Colonel radioed this update with his situation report to Site R.

The next day, it was snowing again and seemed as dark as ever. In fact, it snowed violently for two weeks straight. It was like someone had blown out the Colonel's candle; I never saw old man down before in my life, even with all that happened with the impacts. But during those weeks he lost that fire in his eyes. This was a change from the eternal optimist he normally was.

But finally, the snow stopped. On crutches, I had started doing the daily checks of the weather to ease the blow to the Colonel.

I had gotten up in the middle of the night and used my crutches to hobble to the cave entrance. I opened the door just to get some fresh air and take a leak; the cave smelled like a barn with all the animals. I was amazed to see that the wind had died down again significantly. In the absence of wind, the quiet was eerie, and it was dark, of course. I then looked up and almost fell over, barely keeping balance on my crutches. High above in the night sky was what looked like a full moon—heavily clouded, but still visibly peeking through the clouds with a ring surrounding the disk.

I watched the sky for about five minutes, and then Kaitlin came looking for me. "Honey are you all right?" she said, putting her arms around me.

I just pointed up and she started to cry. It was the moon.

I said, "Let's wait a little while before we tell the Colonel; I do not want to get his hopes up again. He has been in a depression since the false alert two weeks ago."

Needless to say, neither Kaitlin nor I slept the rest of that night, as we lay in our double bed; little Bobby lay between us in bed. I felt the same anticipation, waiting for morning, that I felt when I was a kid waiting for Christmas morning to come.

At about 8 a.m., not able to wait any longer, I hobbled to the door again for another look outside. The wind and cold hit me hard, but there was light! Not a lighter shade of gray, but real light! I could see the trees and rocks around the cave for the first time since the day of the impacts—without a flashlight. It takes a lot of concentration to navigate on my crutches, and I almost fell down four times trying to get back to the cabin as quickly as I could.

All I could utter when I got there was "Light!"

Everyone but me and the babies ran back to the cave door.

"The weather is cold and nasty, but by gosh there is light," was all the Colonel could say. The fire in his eyes had returned. I was glad to have my dad back again. We all needed the strong man that he was.

****

Johnnie woke up to the normal routine of getting the fire going again and then heating water for oatmeal and hot chocolate. He then went outside to get more firewood. Johnnie could not believe it, there was actually light out; it was not super bright, but it was obvious there was real light in the sky. The houses around him that he'd never really seen were in view.

Sometimes the smallest thing can bring immense optimism and hope. Johnnie had his spirits lifted tenfold for the first time in a year.

****

The president spoke to the astronauts to confirm that the dark gray clouds were now turning to white clouds, but with the surface still hard to distinguish. But at least something was happening. The weather however, was still cold, inhospitable, and unforgiving.

The President was advised that NORAD in the Cheyenne Mountain complex had rigged up some type of antenna and could soon begin normal radio transmissions again once everything was more permanently tied down. Reports said that 238 people were still alive at Cheyenne Mountain. Even with aggressive antibiotics and treatment, the mysterious flu that had hit just before the impact had killed a few people in the year since the impacts. General Hawk at NORAD said they had actually got a couple of the geo-synch spy satellites on line and were waiting for things to clear up a little more to check out the earth's surface.

****

It took another two months, until April 2013, before there was full sunlight. With the warmth of the sun on the oceans, there also came additional precipitation in the form of snow. But the temperature was now averaging in the twenties in Leechburg. The Colonel made a trek to his house, to look around a bit.

The snow-covered land looked more like a scene from the movie *The Day After Tomorrow* than anything he could recognize as his yard. At the house, in the deep drifts, the Colonel entered through a second floor window. He fashioned snowshoes out of two wicker lawn chairs from the garage, affixing them to his boots with clothesline. He also had to find his sunglasses; the sun shining on the snow made it almost impossible to see. The Colonel then walked to Kevin and Jennifer's house.

The walk was anything but easy. The Colonel struggled, walking atop the deep slow constantly stepping on the opposite snowshoe or sinking down too deep in the snow.

The roadway was only discernable because there were no trees coming up through the snow. The Colonel had to lift a telephone line that crossed the road; the snow was that deep. He nevertheless enjoyed the walk in the bright sunlight beneath the sapphire-blue sky. What amazed him most was the absence of noise. When the wind did not blow, there was absolute silence. The mile and a half walk to Kevin and Jennifer's house took him an hour and a half.

Jennifer was now visibly pregnant at four months, with the classic "bump" talked about in the gossip magazines. Kevin and Jennifer appeared no worse for wear for a year plus in the dark, alone. They were in good spirits for the Colonel's visit.

The Colonel was the last person they had seen in well over a year, before the snow had gotten too bad and everyone had had to hunker down and wait out the weather. During his visit with Kevin and Jennifer, the Colonel gave the couple about twenty-five more nine-volt batteries for their walkie-talkie.

After about two hours at the Rock's house, the Colonel made his way back to the cave. During the mile-plus walk back to the cave, the weather turned windy and snowy again, with the sky going from blue to gray. The Colonel stepped into the cave just as it started torrentially snowing. The Colonel realized that just because there is light, the weather conditions were still just as dangerous. He pondered on the fact that had he had stayed even a half-hour longer at the Rock's than he had, he might not have made it back alive.

The Colonel made a mental note to make a better pack of survival supplies, if he were to make this outing again; he just got plain lucky this time.

****

Johnnie used the daylight to assess his situation better. He walked around Ford Cliff looking for other survivors but did not see any other than Bill, Mary, and the kids. He did notice a smoke plume cutting into the sapphire blue sky across the Allegheny River from roughly where the Armstrong County Memorial

Hospital was situated; he suspected it might be from the folks he met there last year. But that was an eight-mile walk in the wrong direction through six to eight feet of snow.

Johnnie then walked in the direction of Crooked Creek to assess the road conditions for when he decided to make his way to Leechburg. The snowy landscape was too difficult to traverse in a timely manner, plus he would most likely still have to find a way to ford the torrent of water that crossed downstream from the Crooked Creek emergency overflow.

Johnnie did not get too far, when the weather took a turn for the worse. He headed back for the house. He also suddenly realized that he was almost snowblind and had a splitting migraine headache.

Once inside, Johnnie could barely see anything, and what he could see had a reddish-pink tinge to it. He was suffering from minor snowblindness. He took several aspirins for the headache and his snowblindness cleared up in a couple of hours.

CHAPTER 21

The Warming

"A lot of people like snow. I find it to be an unnecessary freezing of water."
CARL REINER

The snowstorm Johnnie just avoided raged on for ten more days. It was now May 3, 2013. The temperature was actually warming—it had reached the freezing point—but this was no solace for Johnnie, waiting out the storm. The snow was coming down wet, heavy, and deep. Johnnie awoke to a loud crash—part of the neighboring house's carport next door collapsed from the weight of the snow. The old company-made house that Johnnie lived in held up well.

When Johnnie attempted to open the door, snow was two-thirds of the way to the top of it. To get out the front door, he had to make snowshoes out of paneling tied to his boots. Movement was slow and very cumbersome. Through the snow and perpetual mist Johnnie made his way to Bill's place to check up on them. Johnnie smiled as he shook off the two inches of wet snow that had accumulated on his jacket from his short walk and asked how they were doing.

Mary said, "We are surviving; both our front and back porches collapsed from the snow, but the main house is holding," while she took Johnnie's coat. The kids looked at his snowshoes with complete wonder.

Johnnie ate lunch with them and made his way back to his home. The grandchildren always enjoyed Johnnie's visits; Johnnie had become part father figure and part big brother to them. He always took time to get down on his knees and play with them.

****

On June 2, the Colonel checked the weather outside the cave, just as he did almost every day. The temperature was now 38 degrees. It was sleeting, not snowing. With at least ten feet of snow on the ground, it would need to warm up substantially for any of the snow to melt, he realized. Today, they would celebrate little Bobby's first birthday with pear halves and a canned fruit cake.

****

General Hawk looked at the reconnaissance photos from the spy reconnaissance satellites. Almost all the earth's land surfaces were now covered with snow; only the equator and the tropics showed some areas without snow. The impact zone in the Pacific still spewed out steam, and lots of it at that. The intelligence team at the mountain looked for the impact zones of the three meteor showers the space station had observed months earlier.

The spy satellites were good—they could read a license plate on a car if they had the exact coordinates to go by. But they did not have anything that specific to go on; the intel team had to meticulously look at ten-mile swaths of land at a time.

One of the airmen on the team mentioned something to the effect of "finding a needle amongst a *thousand* haystacks,"

But with time as an inexhaustible commodity now, the team endured in their meticulous search for some sign of the three mysterious showers.

WITHOUT WARNING

****

On July 4, the rain came down in absolute buckets. The temperature was now in the high forties. Johnnie looked out the door at the virtual waterfalls coming off the roof of the house; the gutters were long gone and the basement flooded almost to the top of the steps. The snow was melting, and melting quickly. Johnnie suspected the Allegheny was flooding again. The entire area seemed to be in a perpetual veil of fog from the rain and melting snow. After two weeks of almost constant rain, the temperatures were now in the fifties during the day and flirting with freezing at night. The snow was nearly all gone now. With the moisture in the air, it was bone-chilling at night when Johnnie made his way back from visits with Bill, Mary, and the kids.

Johnnie took a walk early one day in late July and was rewarded with the most spectacular sunrise. The morning sun lit the horizon up like a bright red explosion. The valley still held a residual fog, as sunbeams pierced through it with pin-pricks of light at infrequent intervals. It had been about a year and a half since the impacts, but the town of Ford Cliff looked like it had sat abandoned for decades—like one of those History Channel shows, *Life without People*, Johnnie thought.

Debris was strewn everywhere from the snow and rain. The rain had not quite let up and was spitting random drops through the sunbeams. Mary opened the door to the view of a rainbow behind Johnnie.

Johnnie told them, "I am going to try to get home soon, when and if the weather lets up just a little more." Bill and Mary understood his motivations but secretly wondered if he would ever really find what he was looking for. The grandkids would miss Johnnie; he was the closest thing to normalcy they had known since before the impacts. And soon, Johnnie would say goodbye to them.

****

On July 29, 2013, the Colonel found the snow had melted enough that he could walk up to his house again without snowshoes. The only snow left was in the big drifts that had now melted down to manageable size. The snow drifts did not quite seem so intimidating now.

The Colonel and Missy made their way to the Rocks house to check on the soon-to-be mother. The Colonel noted some lingering snow drifts and other debris that would need cleared off the road before he got the truck out of the garage and running. But, that was another day.

Jennifer was now almost eight months along in her pregnancy. Missy gave her the best exam she could. As far as Missy could tell, everything appeared normal with Jennifer.

Grabbing her expanded stomach, Jennifer said, "I am more than ready to have this baby."

Missy jokingly said, "you can't put a flow chart to these kind of things," remembering a quote from Johnnie about planning out her getting pregnant.

Missy had spent a lot of time recently studying medical issues in the various books and periodicals, given her new role as pseudo-doctor for the group. After the short visit, they decided that Missy would pack a bag and come back in a couple days and stay with the Kevin and Jennifer until Jennifer had the baby.

****

"This is Jim Stockwell. –Bob, are you there?— over,"

The Colonel responded, "Good morning, Mr. President, how are you all doing?"

The two men had talked about the Colonel's plans to send Missy to the farmer's house for the birth of the baby. The president said for him to drop her off and get back to the cave within the next thirty-six hours. From the spy satellites photos, the

NORAD team was now able to crudely predict weather as part of the routine between NORAD and Site R. Dick Ford was able to supplement these weather reports as well from his vantage point in space.

The president said, "Another monster storm with hurricane force winds is sweeping across the United States. The Pacific impact zone is still kicking out hurricane-like storms from the massive heat it is still emitting. From the scientists' best estimates at NORAD, the climate will heat up over the next year," he said. "Pennsylvania will eventually have a climate more like Alabama's from the greenhouse gases released at the Pacific impact site, and it will take centuries, if ever, for these same gases to return to pre-impact levels."

He continued, "If this rock had struck almost anywhere else in the world, we'd be in an ice age for centuries. And between the two options, I guess this is one of life's very small but useful serendipities," the president quipped.

CHAPTER 22
The Journey Home

"Home is a place you grow up wanting to leave, and grow old wanting to get back to."
JOHN ED PEARCE

Johnnie woke up to a sunny day. This was the first time there was no real snow on the ground other than random snow drifts. The spooky thing about the day was the absolute silence—not a bird or even a breeze to stir things. Johnnie got his pack—he had readied it days earlier—and made his way to Bill and Mary's to make his farewells to the family. The kids both cried, along with Mary. Bill just shook his hand and wished him well.

Johnnie said, "I'll come back and visit you all someday soon, don't worry," fighting back his own emotions.

As the kids watched through the cracked living room window, Johnnie walked out the door and disappeared into the landscape. The grandkids kept waving until Johnnie was out of sight.

The air had a spring smell to it most of the time, but as Johnnie passed some of the houses, he could smell the distinct odor of decaying bodies. He made it to the Crooked Creek overflow with no problem; this was as far as he had made it last time, just after the impacts. From there, however, the water still flowed swiftly where the roadway once had been. The water was brown and debris-filled.

Johnnie walked up to the lake, to look for a means to ford the emergency overflow spillway. To his surprise, he saw all kinds of debris jammed across the overflow entrance, with water flowing under it through several deep gullies cut away by the water. The debris of trees, roots, buildings, and many other things made a kind of haphazard bridge across the water, albeit a very dangerous one to cross.

Johnnie spent four hours getting across the debris bridge, with every move painstakingly calculated. He almost fell into the raging water below several times, and grabbed at some loose roots and branches. When he finally made it across the emergency spillway, he lay on the shoreline for an hour, soaking in the sun. The stress of crossing the debris bridge had taken a physical as well as a mental toll.

Johnnie made his way to the actual dam of Crooked Creek. The water was within feet of the top of the dam, but the dam itself had held through it all. *I'll be damned, the dam held,* Johnnie thought to himself, no pun intended as he half laughed.

He went into the dam control tower and took a look around the console room. Johnnie hit the switch for the back-up power and an old diesel engine generator fired to life.

How strange is that? he thought.

The sound of the generator roared through the valley, breaking the absolute silence. The lights on the control panel soon lit up in the dam operations center.

Johnnie then worked the levers for the normal spillway. Apparently the opening was clogged with debris and he broke the clog by opening the spillway gates further. Surprisingly, he heard a distant siren sound, and then the din of water flowing. Johnnie walked over and looked down below and saw water gushing out of the normal spillway. He then went back to the control tower and turned off the power and walked across the top of the Crooked Creek dam and eventually made his way back to Route 66.

The road barely looked like a road anymore except in places. Johnnie came to another stream that had washed out the road just down the road from the remnants of an old warehouse surrounded by Canadian hemlocks. With darkness coming, Johnnie set up camp beside the beaten-down warehouse and built a large fire from the abundance of firewood in the area.

There was no moon that night, as Johnnie looked up and saw the most stars he had ever seen in his life. *What a show*, he thought, remembering his nights in the middle of the Iraqi desert years ago.

The temperature quickly cooled down again with darkness and a cool breeze enveloped the valley. Johnnie also saw several falling stars. Then he fell asleep to the soothing sound of water running in the distance.

The next morning, Johnnie looked for a means to ford the stream that had cut through the roadway. After a couple of hours, he found a tree that bridged the stream about a half mile up out of the valley. Johnnie kept walking back down the hill until he got back to Route 66; he finally made it to the Gilpin Township line and was then only seven miles from the Colonel's house.

He decided to stay on the main road versus taking a shortcut through the woods or back roads to the Colonel's house. Johnnie saw smoke in the distance, near the Lingrow Farm. But it was getting late and Johnnie stayed on track, anxious to get to the Colonel's house.

He finally made it to the New Schenley Road, and was now four miles from the Colonel's house. The weather looked foreboding up ahead. Johnnie hurried down the road, making it to the Old Schenley Road. As he crested the hill on the Old Schenley Road, his heart almost sank. There in front of him was what appeared to be Missy's car on the side of the road. He ran over to the car, opened the door, and looked in the glove box and confirmed that it was registered to his wife. But there was no body; maybe, just maybe, Missy was alright.

As Johnnie stood by Missy's car holding the registration, the initial wind surge from the massive storm front that was cutting across the United States hit him. He was not even a mile and a half from home when the storm hit came from out of nowhere in all its fury. Given the absolute ferocity of the storm, Johnnie knew he could not survive long in it out in the elements; he had to find shelter, and find it fast.

****

Missy had been at the farmer's house for twenty-four hours. It was a good thing she had come when she did, with the storm on its way. Jennifer had gone into early labor that morning, after she'd taken the dog out and slipped and fell in the mud. Missy had her lie down in bed and prepared to deliver the baby. *What if the baby is breeched?* she worriedly thought to herself. She didn't know how to do a C-section, and she knew that attempting one would almost certainly mean death for the mother and the child. Missy quickly regained her cool and told herself to deal with things as they came.

The storm hit the farmer's house like a runaway train; the sounds from the storm were intense. Just then, as if her body knew from some sort of primordial instinct, Jennifer went into full labor. She screamed from the pain of the contractions. Kevin was hysterical, seeing his wife in pain. Missy ordered him out of the room until he could calm down; all Kevin could do was sit downstairs on the sofa biting his nails as the storm rolled over their house and his wife gave birth.

Kevin could hear Missy say through the screaming, "One more push, girlfriend."

Just then, there was a knock at the farmer's door, as Jennifer screamed in pain and the baby crowned. Totally miffed, the farmer opened the door to a man who looked like he had gone fifteen rounds with Apollo Creed. "Can I come in," the man said.

Kevin said, "This is not a good time," hearing his wife screaming, but let the man in with the raging storm outside.

Just then, they both heard the sound of a newborn wailing. A figure emerged, looking over the upstairs banister, holding a crying baby. It was Missy. She almost fainted but realized she had to keep her cool.

"Johnnie! My God, you're alive!"

Missy went back into the bedroom and handed the new mother her baby girl, and then hugged Johnnie. They both cried as they held each other. In a world that seemed so wrong, for one moment, things seemed right. All the explanations could wait. Missy then told him that their baby, Anna, was doing well. She said their daughter was with Kaitlin and her cousin Bobby at the Colonel's cave. Missy then worked to get the new mom and baby relaxed and rested.

The storm raged outside for the next five days with Johnnie and Missy oblivious to it all, wrapped up in each other's company. They told each other their stories of the last year of their lives.

CHAPTER 23
Census

"The true test of civilization is not the census, nor the size of the cities, nor the crops, but the kind of man that the country turns out."
RALPH WALDO EMERSON

The President was informed by Chip that they had taken two of the Osprey aircraft out of their underground storage bunker near Site R and could have them operational in a couple days. The underground hanger was added to the facility following the attacks of September 11, 2001, in case of a terrorist attack on the East Coast, and as a back-up plan to extract the leadership of Washington in a pinch.

"The chopper pilot and co-pilot from Marine One are reading the manuals on how to fly the Ospreys," Chip told President Stockwell.

****

The Colonel could hardly believe the news about Johnnie when he got word over the walkie-talkie from Kevin. In the Colonel's report to Site R, he passed along word of the other survivors Johnnie had met since the impacts. With the news of survivors, the president immediately appointed the Colonel regional commander of western Pennsylvania and charged him with conducting a complete census of the area for other survivors, as soon as the weather improved. The Colonel accepted his new post.

"Regis," the President said, "you will be charged with relaying communications for the Colonel, your dad, as he makes his surveys, to Site R and other locations if they come on line."

"Yes, Mr. President," was all I could say, hardly believing I was talking to the president of the United States. I was nervous talking to the president, even under these unique circumstances, and I stammered slightly in my response. At the time, I secretly thought it was sort of kooky—me a signal officer—but a lot would happen as I held this post over the months to come.

After changing the truck's oil and charging its battery, the Colonel got his truck running again in short order. It was now September 2013, and the weather kept throwing one surprise after another in the form of violent and/or freak storms, along with the most petrifying lightning shows ever seen. If there was global warming on the horizon, it was not happening quite yet. The weather would dip back below freezing most nights.

The Colonel had Johnnie ride shotgun with him as they started their survey missions. The first job was to clear debris out of the road just to get to the Rocks' house. The Colonel's truck was fitted with a mobile CB, plus the cave was fitted with an old CB base station re-using the old "Starduster" antenna that was on the Colonel's house; Pap put it there years before. The Colonel and Johnnie loaded chain saws, ropes, axes, shovels, and other gear in the truck bed to clear the roads with.

It took several hours to clear the road between the farmer's house and the cave; Johnnie drove Jennifer and the baby to the cave to be with the other women and babies. Kevin then joined Johnnie and the Colonel as they cleared a path to the main road, Route 66.

The first day of work netted only another mile past the farmer's house. The next big obstacle was to clear about twenty trees around a steep curve on the New Schenley Road. That evening, I got the debriefing from the Colonel, wrote up the report, and radioed the report to Site R.

****

Site R started receiving reports from Offutt Air Force Base near Omaha, Nebraska, that September. Apparently, the folks in the Strategic Air Command bunker survived the firestorm: General James Lawson and his staff, approximately 180 men and women who were on duty and saved from the firestorm by the bunker facility's blast doors. They had just managed to get a radio up and running in the last few days, scrounging old parts from around the facility.

General Lawson said that the entire area around Offutt Air Force was devoid of anything; a complete wasteland. Anything combustible had burned away in the first hour after the impact. He said he had enough food for several more months but would need supplies no later than the end of the year. He said, "We have several working vehicles in the bunker garage. If we can get the big doors to it open, we can get out of the local area to forage for additional supplies, which are much needed."

CHAPTER 24

Anomaly

"Do what you fear and fear disappears."
DAVID JOSEPH SCHWARTZ

A young airman at NORAD combed over the spy satellite images. He thought he saw a white speck on one of them, and the speck on the image looked out of place compared to the surrounding landscape detail. The images appeared somewhere in the center of southern Iowa. The Airman noted the exact coordinates for the location and asked for refined images of the area in question. Since the satellites were also used for weather reports and by other analysts, it would take a day or two to get the requested images.

The young airman thought it was probably just a pixelization of the image, but decided to pursue it just the same, to be thorough. After putting in the Satcom request for the refined image, the airman went on with his mile by mile search for the suspected meteor strikes in Iowa. The terrain in Iowa had other pockmarks from secondary debris that rained down in the hours after the Pacific impact, making the search even more troublesome.

****

Gunny Frank Sergeant Joyce had the remaining cadets at the Institute charge the cannons. The cadet's fired three volleys at high noon from the canon as a signal to the cadet company's dispersed throughout the Shenandoah Valley to send reps to meet at VMI. The concussions thundered through the valleys in the dead silence. Gunny Sergeant Joyce had another group of cadets build a large fire on neighboring house mountain for the next three days.

Within a week, Sergeant Joyce confirmed received envoys from all the dispersed companies. Gunny Joyce was pleased to learn all but five cadets were alive. Most of the cadet enclaves had also taken in or helped the survivors in their area.

****

The Colonel, Johnnie, and Kevin got past the big tree fall on the New Schenley Road and were on Route 66, clearing the roadway. They had decided to check out the area where Johnnie had seen smoke when he was walking home from Ford Cliff.

"The main road appears to require a lot less work to clear," the Colonel said to no one in particular.

Within an hour, they had made it to where Johnnie had seen smoke, just past the 1844 Restaurant near Lingrow Farm. All of them were amazed at how the restaurant looked none the worse for wear for all that happened, except for the cracked windows. The old structure truly proved the test of time.

With the sky gray and heavy ground fog with a spitting rain, none of the men could see the smoke Johnnie had reported when walking to the Colonel's cave. Finally, Kevin said, "Honk the horn three times and repeat several times. That should get anyone's attention, if anyone's around."

The Colonel made the long blasts on the truck's horn. They got no response, so he proposed they eat their lunch before heading back to the cave.

Suddenly, from out of the fog emerged an emaciated middle-aged man. He was pointing a rifle at them. Johnnie said to the Colonel and Kevin, "We have company, men," as he put down his container of cold Dinty Moore beef stew.

All of them moved slowly and kept their cool. Johnnie put on his charm, smiled and said, "Hi" and finally the man lowered his rifle. "What's your name, pal?" Johnnie asked the man.

"Smittie, they call me Smittie," the man said. He asked if the Colonel and Johnnie had any extra food. The Colonel said, "Sure, we'll give you all we have in the truck," and gave the man a reassuring nod.

The man appeared to be almost in shock from all that had happened since the day of the impacts. He had the classic thousand-yard stare the Colonel remembered from his days in combat in Vietnam. As they talked, Smittie told them how his immediate family—wife and two kids, his parents, and other relatives, sixteen people in all—had doubled up in their underground home the day of the impact. All survived the day but his parents later died of the flu or something, and his niece died from her type II diabetes, having run out of insulin a few days after the impacts.

He said they did not have a lot of provisions left and had been scavenging houses in the area. "Everyone else in the area above ground had died from the heat wave," Smittie said, his face reflecting the losses he felt. "Lately, we have had a hard time finding food, and we are all too weak to walk any distance anymore," he lamented. He said that one of his nephews was very close to death.

Barring bad weather, the Colonel said they would come back with more provisions the next day. The Colonel knew they would need to give food slowly to the families for them to survive. Too much food eaten too quickly would make them sick; the Colonel had seen this on a humanitarian mission to Somalia in 1993, with the Pennsylvania Guard. He had watched as the NGO humanitarian organization dispersed small quantities of food to the refugees.

Johnnie radioed a report to me over the CB. After spending some time with the Rock family, the Colonel, Johnnie, and Kevin scoped out the road going in the other direction towards Leechburg. It would need a little work clearing the debris to get back into town, but it was doable.

That evening, Dad, Missy, and I started readying the provisions to take to the Rocks the next day. The Colonel also rounded up another CB radio and batteries to give them. Getting them back to good health would take several weeks to several months, if they were lucky. After finding more survivors, our optimism was growing that things just might get better someday.

I radioed a report to Site R practically as soon as I got the info from the Colonel. The president came on the radio and related his thanks for the update. He sounded upbeat with the latest report.

CHAPTER 25

Refined Pictures

"In this world of change, nothing which comes stays, and nothing which goes is lost."
ANNE SOPHIE SWETCHINE

The airman checked the updated satellite reconnaissance photos he'd just received for the white dot he'd spotted earlier. The magnified images showed a cylindrical object about the size of a minivan on the ground. The top side of the cylinder was pure white and the bottom part, as much as could be seen, was charred black. The object was probably discolored from entry into earth's atmosphere and not from the firestorm at the time of the impact or it would have charred all over.

This object looked out of place in the middle of a charred field as well. The airman called out to the intelligence officer on duty to look at the recon photo. She could not make heads or tails of what the object was, either, but she was certain it was not a natural feature of the land. Since the Cheyenne Mountain complex only had voice communications with Site R, the information was related to the signal officer at Site R in a sit rep. Photos of the object would have to wait for delivery by a courier at some point.

Because the airman knew what to look for now, he kept up his search for objects in the areas adjacent to the first object.

By that evening, he had found almost twenty-five similar white "specks" on the panned out reconnaissance photos. These anomalies would require additional close-in photos for complete validation of the specks.

The airman started plotting them on a map and very quickly started to see a recognizable pattern appear: the objects were equally spaced, about eighteen kilometers apart. In fact, the airman was able to find additional dots by filling in the open spots and guessing the location of the next object, until a circle stretching 180 kilometers wide emerged. The object locations had a spoke-and-wheel look to them. By this time, the senior intelligence officer was coordinating all efforts to identify the specks in Iowa; she also had her team looking in Russia and Africa for the same kind of anomalies.

****

"There's no doubt sir, the objects came from space after the impact," General Hawk explained to the president. "The objects appear to be made of metal or tiles, and are not random pieces of rock," the general went on to say.

"What exactly are you trying to say, general?"

"Mr. President, these objects are no accident, they look like some type of landing pods or probes, deliberately sent here, sir," General Hawk said.

"Get me answers, General Hawk. I want them now, I want to understand what we are dealing with here," the president ordered. "Get me your best guess or theory as to why they are here, Steve," he continued in a calmer voice.

"Yes, Mr. President, we will do our absolute best, sir—over," the General said in a reassuring voice.

****

The Colonel, Johnnie, Kevin, and Missy went to the Smiths' the next day. Missy examined everyone. All were underweight, but appeared to be fit enough to fully recover in due time. Kevin stayed with Missy and the Colonel and Johnnie drove into town. With about two hour's effort, the Colonel and Johnnie cleared a path down Route 66 into Leechburg. In town, they loaded the truck with what salvageable supplies they could find, even though a lot of the cans did not have labels on them anymore. The Colonel and Johnnie both knew a lot of the cans would start to corrode soon, especially the cans exposed to the elements.

Johnnie talked the Colonel into stopping by his house before they picked up Missy and Kevin. Johnnie walked through the shell of what was left of their home, finding some salvageable items in the closets. He picked up several photo albums from inside their dresser, and Missy's and his wedding album. Johnnie also got his gun collection out of the gun safe, as well as ammo. The high-end gun safe he had bought the Christmas before the impacts had held up well through it all.

By the time the men got back to Smithville, Missy had examined everyone. One of the Smith teenagers served as her assistant. Missy was surprised at how quick of a study he was, as well as the absolute compassion this young man had shown caring for his people. In another time, this young man would be a natural as a nurse or even a doctor.

CHAPTER 26
Extraction

"Without mission, there's no purpose. Without vision, there's no destination. Without values, there are no guiding principles."
PAUL THORTON

The flight crew loaded the Osprey with fuel and supplies for its cross-country trip to Iowa and back on a crisp September day. The Osprey's auxiliary power units (APUs) were already running and the extraction team awaited their departure. The Marine One pilots went through the lengthy pre-flight checklist. The NORAD commander, General Hawk, had a hunch the people survived at Wright Patterson Air Force Base in Ohio.

Wright Patterson AFB had a huge network of underground research facilities, with many scientists most likely on duty working in them on the day of the impacts. Some of these folks must surely have survived, the general surmised, and his plan included a stop at Wright Patterson on the way to Iowa. Ideally, the extraction team would return whatever was found to Wright Patterson for investigation.

The large propellers started turning on the Osprey, cracking in the air, and soon they were at a throttle level just below the aircraft's ability to obtain lift. The noise and wind made it hard for the team scurrying around to communicate. The flight to Wright Patterson would take a little over an hour and a half.

****

The extra fuel was strapped down in several tanks in the cargo area of the Osprey, which now had the distinct smell of JP4 jet fuel. The team of soldiers readied for the extraction mission squeezed in between the gear on the cargo seats. The engines roared as the pilots throttled the Osprey to maximum RPMs and the plane took off vertically, like a helicopter. The team tried to get as comfortable as possible on the red cargo-net seating. At a safe distance above the ground, the propellers turned from horizontal to vertical and the plane slowly moved forward, gaining speed. The president watched all the happenings from an outbuilding near the small tarmac; he continued to watch until the plane was completely out of sight.

****

The Colonel and Johnnie were in town scrounging supplies to help the Smith family on that day, September 12, 2013. They had already found enough canned goods to keep the Smith compound going for almost a year. They had set up two additional houses in a housing development near the underground house to give the extended family members some much needed breathing room. In pre-impact times, Smittie's underground house was the joke of the neighborhood. He had built as part of the green movement to save energy.

The Colonel also found bags of fine cracked corn at the Apollo Milling feed store outside of town. The plan was to start hatching chicks soon to expand the flock of chickens. The Colonel had set up the chicken coops just outside the cave entrance. Once the hens had been let out of the cave for a couple hours each day in their pens, they had started laying eggs again. The fresh air and sunlight had a positive effect on them.

The Colonel heard a noise he had not heard since before the impacts: an airplane. The Colonel knew Site R was going to take one of the Ospreys for a flight, but the president had not elaborated on the details. The Colonel recognized the Osprey immediately and waved. He was not sure if he had been seen; however, the plane did wag its wings as it flew over Leechburg.

****

The Marine One pilot flew lower than normal to see the ground more easily. Besides extracting the pod in Iowa, the president had asked if the pilots could look for signs of survivors by watching for smoke from fires. Surprisingly, there was actually smoke coming from chimneys at irregular intervals from Site R to Ohio, though much less frequently once they were in eastern Ohio, the pilot noted.

Per the plan, the Osprey set down at Wright Patterson AFB near the main entrance to the underground complex. The pilots found a clear spot amongst the shells of burned out vehicles to set the Osprey down on the pavement. Several men approached the Osprey as the propellers throttled down. The Marine One co-pilot kept the APU running on the Osprey as the pilot/commander of the extraction team exited the chopper. One of the men who approached the Osprey introduced himself as the base's vice commander and lead scientist, a bird Air Force colonel, Dave Fowler; he said there were survivors in the underground complex, with the overall leader being a senior civilian executive. He said there were also several senior officers and various civilian scientists as well as other support staff, and even some family members and children in the underground complex. The vice commander said there were 312 survivors in all.

"The main task of the survivors has been us just surviving," the vice commander said.

After walking through a maze of tunnels, the Marine One officer finally met with the senior person in charge of the base, a senior executive service employee, George Vulkanburg, appointed under the previous administration. The Marine One senior pilot asked if he and his other most senior officers could meet in private to discuss their mission to Iowa.

Several other members on the Osprey team set up a radio in the underground command post. The scientists at Wright Patterson already had an established a 110-volt power source from an experimental nuclear fusion experiment, making things much easier, but they had no working radio at this point.

The Osprey team had just gotten the antenna up outside and the radio came to life; the radio was operational before the senior officials finished their private meeting. The plane's support team and scientists had good communications going between Wright Patterson and Site R when the Marine One senior pilot exited the private meeting room with the senior civilian executive and staff from their talks.

Cheers broke out at Site R when they heard of the survivors at the military base in Ohio. The president heard the first transmission as it came into the Site R command center; he now spent the majority of his time in the communications room.

As the Mr. Vulcanburg watched the Osprey throttle up, his number two, the vice commander, Dave Fowler, immediately started barking out orders to prepare to work on a reverse engineering project for a piece of equipment. A lot of the scientists at the base were used to receiving odd deliveries in U-Hauls in the middle of the night. Most of their efforts were designed to reverse engineer various foreign technologies. No one asked how these objects were obtained from their sources; not asking was just one of those unspoken rules.

Before the Osprey was even airborne for Iowa, a supply building was already being readied for the incoming arrival. The flight from Wright Patterson to Iowa would take another three hours. As the plane crossed into Indiana the effects of the firestorm became ever more evident. At the Iowa border, everything on the surface was completely burned out of existence. When the plane reached the final coordinates, the white object easily came into view in the middle of a burned-out cornfield.

The plane set down in the field within fifty feet of the object; the pilot and co-pilot had to compensate for a high crosswind when they touched down and the crew were violently jolted from the unexpected down draft.

The object was definitely not natural to the surrounding landscape. The extraction team looked out at the charred Iowa landscape when they exited the Osprey; the scene was so foreign looking, it did not even look like they were on planet earth.

The pod appeared to have hatches in various locations on its surface, and to be decorated with some unknown hieroglyphic-type writing. It also looked like it had solar cells or sensors of some sort. The team was able to roll the pod over—it was surprisingly light.

Within an hour of putting up all seats, dumping some extra gear, and squeezing everyone into the plane, the team loaded the pod into the Osprey and lifted off Iowa's burnt soil. The pilot set a course for Wright Patterson Air Force Base, Ohio. As they got closer to Ohio, the team was able to radio Wright Patterson with a report. The message was then relayed from Ohio to Site R with a coded phrase that would let the staff at Site R know the extraction team had retrieved the object.

It was almost dark when the Osprey set down at the Wright Patterson AFB hanger complex; the crimson sun hung low on the horizon. Waiting at the landing pad was a team of almost forty scientists and technicians ready to start their study of the object. After the receiving team unloaded the pod, the Marine One pilots immediately took off for Site R. At the same time that the object was being unloaded, the Osprey team refueled the aircraft, keeping the down time to a minimum.

ANTHONY G. SHEA, JR.

The flight from Ohio to Site R was uneventful and the Osprey landed at the site as if this were a routine sortie. A team stood by on the tarmac to tow the plane back into the hardened bunker. The president waited at the hangar door for a personal debrief from the Marine One pilots as soon as they exited the aircraft.

****

The sun was shining, and the weather cooling somewhat on September 17, 2013. Winter weather would come again, but in its normal form, all hoped. Even with the warming after the sun appeared again, not all the snow had completely melted in shaded and large drift areas. The temperature never got above 60 degrees in the daytime, even in the bright sunlight, and it usually dipped to about freezing overnight, even in July and August.

Johnnie and the Colonel spent the second half of the month helping the extended Smith family ready for winter; they had expanded their supply-gathering efforts to the Allegheny Township's Giant Eagle, K-Mart, and Save a Lot. They cleared the road north on Route 66 to Ford Cliff and Kittanning. One part of the road required fashioning a bridge out of logs to get past the gulley cut by the Crooked Creek emergency spillway. They finally made it up to Ford Cliff and visited the old couple, Bill and Mary, and their grandchildren. The children immediately ran up to Johnnie and hugged him when he stepped out of the Colonel's truck. All in all, Bill, Mary, and the kids were doing well.

The Colonel connected immediately with Bill. After everyone was caught up on all the news, the Colonel asked if the couple wanted to move down to Gilpin Township with the other survivors at the newly formed Smith village. Without much thought, Bill and Mary readily agreed. The Colonel said they would prepare an abandoned house for them and would come back in a couple of weeks. The Colonel gave the couple an old mobile CB radio, several car batteries, and an antenna so they could keep in contact.

CHAPTER 27
Reverse Engineering

"All truths are easy to understand once they are discovered; the point is to discover them"
GALILEO GALILEI

The group of scientists at Wright Patterson AFB started their work on the pod within minutes of its arrival at the base. Luckily, they already had protocols in place for the processes used to reverse engineer technologies given to them. Within hours, the Wright Patterson team had measured the external object and weighed it. The scientist then tested the external material for its atomic element composition. The material did not register as any known atomic element found on earth.

The surface of the pod did have a composition similar to the space shuttle's heat resistant tiles, and the pod's tiles even had better thermodynamic properties. The items that looked like solar cells appeared to have just that purpose, as well as having some type of sensors, possibly for environmental monitoring. Another team of sociologists and anthropologists researched the markings on the pod, with no success. The markings were like a kind of boilerplate repeating itself at several points on the pod, but matched no known lettering schema archived in the scientists' extensive database.

ANTHONY G. SHEA, JR.

The senior civilian at Wright Patterson, George Vulcanburg, contacted the president on Thursday, September 19. He then motioned for all his staff to leave the room. He asked President Stockwell, "Are you with trusted personnel?"

The President answered, "Yes, I am."

"Mr. President, the object that was retrieved is not of our world." George Vulcanburg said this in the most matter-of-fact way.

"What!" exclaimed the president.

"From our preliminary work, we have determined the pod to be alien in nature; the composition of the shell is of a compound not found on earth, but as a theoretical compound on the atomic chart. The solar cells on the surface appear to be just what they seem, however, their micro-circuitry is more complex than anything we have examined here at the lab. The symbology cannot be traced in our databases to any known language from earth by the few sociologists and anthropologists we have on site," he said, looking at the photos of the symbology as he briefed the president.

"Mr. President, I need to request your permission to break through the pod's outer shell to examine the object's inner workings. This will of course permanently damage the object, but we believe it is the only way we can extract its contents and perhaps determine its purpose and origin."

"You have my permission to do whatever is required to find answers regarding the origin of this object," the president said.

"Yes, Mr. President."

"Any ideas why these pods are here?" the president asked.

"Not yet, Mr. President. I could only speculate." the senior civilian spoke cautiously, knowing the president might push him for his speculation.

"Keep me posted on a daily basis regarding your findings," the president said. "I can be summoned any time, day or night, if there's anything of even the remotest significance found—over." The president wanted to leave no doubt about the importance of this subject on his personal radar screen.

"Yes, Mr. President—over," Mr. Vulcanburg said.

CHAPTER 28

Moving Day

"Change is the law of life and those who look only to the past or present are certain to miss the future."

JOHN F. KENNEDY

On Tuesday, October 1, 2013, it snowed about four inches. The team of movers drove to Ford Cliff to move Bill, Mary, and the kids. The Colonel and Johnnie had found an abandoned house suitable for them in Smithville; the house was clean and smelled of pine cleaner and was ready for its new occupants. The windows had plastic neatly installed in them. The Smiths loaded firewood into the garage and all the cabinets had been stocked with food; there was an ample supply of candles, matches, and even spices. A CB was set up for the family to communicate with the other Smith families, and the cave. The Smith kids were excited to actually have other kids to play with. By this point, Missy now had all the family members back to decent health in Smithville.

No one can be expected to easily leave the house they've lived in all their lives. All were careful to be sensitive to the feelings of the old couple as they loaded Bill's and Mary's personal belongings into the truck. The old man knew they could only take a limited number of items and had prepared his wife for this reality. The children each packed a garbage bag full of stuff for their new home. The older couple packed clothes, several photo album, and several other keepsakes. The Colonel and the family squeezed into the truck's heated cab for the ride from Ford Cliff to Smithville. Johnnie and the two other movers huddled in the bed of the truck under a worn tarp with only their heads poking out as they drove back to Smithville. This was the farthest Bill and Mary had traveled since before the impacts. The ride was rough in places where the road had washed out and the Colonel and Johnnie had fixed only enough of it to get through.

When the movers arrived at their new house in Smithville, another team was already in place, waiting to unload the truck. The waiting team had the truck unloaded in fifteen minutes flat. A fire blazed in the fireplace of Bill's and Mary's new abode. Several women had made housewarming gifts for the house's new occupants.

The Smith children took the new kids to play with them. All in all, everything went as smoothly as it could. Bill shook hands with the Colonel and Johnnie and all the movers; Mary gave the entire moving and move-in team a big hug and thanked each of them individually.

****

The cave had grown cramped with so many people in it for the last eighteen months, and it smelled like a barn, with all the animals that shared the space. After several weeks of cleaning and fixing up our old place, Kaitlin and the baby and I moved back home. Johnnie, Missy, and their baby moved to the neighbor's abandoned split level house next to ours and the Colonel's house.

The Colonel and Mom chose to stay in the cave for the time being, but they did move all the animals to coops and pens outside the cave, near the barn. With some replacing of the hosing, Johnnie managed to get a gas well on the Colonels property working again; the houses now all had their fireplaces burning gas logs, and the stoves worked too. The garages were still packed with firewood just in case the gas well had problems.

The Colonel had fashioned a series of field phones between the houses and the cave; he had done the same for the Smiths' housing area as well. The two enclaves communicated between each other by CBs, and the cave to Site R by ham radio.

Johnnie and the Colonel found several survivors in Kittanning and at the Armstrong County hospital—these were the surviors Johnnie had met when he was trying to make his way to the Colonel's house. The Colonel and Johnnie set up these new-found survivors in other abandoned houses near the Smiths. The area was turning into a thriving little village.

CHAPTER 29
Below the Surface

"Doubt is not below knowledge, but above it."
ALAIN RENE LE SAGE

The lead scientist cut through the pod's outer shell at one of the apparent hatches. The pod had a tube down the middle about two feet in diameter. This center tube had the same obvious hatches in all 360 degrees at equal lengths. The center tube also had two spheres half emerging into the center tube at the ends of the tube. A description of the inner components of the pods was radioed to Site R, and the president was immediately advised. Chip attempted to describe the finding to the president as best as he could from the verbal message he received from the Wright Patterson team.

One of the spheres inside the pod was removed and thoroughly examined. When it was opened, it appeared to be like a rover of some sort, similar to one of the rovers the US landed on Mars years earlier. The rover, as the scientists now called it, had round hatches that matched the exact size of the ones inside the tube on the sphere. The rover also had drills on its side, and rollers of some sort to propel them around the ground.

It appeared there was a micro-computer in the rover, and some type of power source; the same solar cells as the pod, only in smaller form, covered the surface of the sphere/rover. Once the sphere/rover was in a warm room for several days, the rover actually lit up and tried to move but was clamped to the table and the room immediately cooled. The rover deactivated itself again, apparently "hibernating." The rover seemed to activate and deactivate by warmth.

When the Wright Patterson scientists opened one of the cylinders inside the main pod, they found some type of biological material; their best guess was that this material was seeds. The team took the various seeds and put them in flower pots and fashioned a greenhouse with sun lights. A guard kept an eye on the greenhouse, and was given the discretion to set the place ablaze in minutes if things went awry. Less than one week after the scientists planted the seeds, a plant stem emerged from one of the pots. It was bluish-green and similar to a mountain laurel bush. The plant could not be identified by the scientists to anything known on earth through plant DNA analysis.

This plant grew at an amazing rate. A stem could be broken off of the bush and placed in water and would form roots within days and be transplantable in a week. Another set of pots germinated two days after the first; the plants looked sort of like grass, possibly wheat, having the same bluish hue as the bush-like plant. The grass produced seeds for new grass, which grew even faster than the original plants.

In about two weeks, the bushy plants had some type of fruit growing on them that were the size and consistency of blueberries. When analyzed, the fruit tested not poisonous by the Wright Patterson Air Force Base chemist, and were found to have amazing antioxidant nutrients and appeared by all accounts completely safe to eat. Eventually, someone took the plunge and ate some of this fruit. It was tasty, and after eating the berries for about a week, the "test subject" actually reported he felt much better.

"Mr. President," reported the Wright Patterson senior civilian George Vulcanburg, "our best guess is that these pods were sent as drones and their contents intended to deploy at some point, probably based on the weather warming, the idea being to propagate the seeds contained in the pods. The seeds are able to germinate in earth soil and they grow very quickly." He explained, "From what we can tell so far, the plants are completely safe to eat, with amazing nutritional value; one of our folks took it upon himself to test the fruit and has had a tremendous change in health—his blood pressure is normal now, his eyesight improved, and he claims to just feel better and have more energy. The man even reported having an increased libido."

****

All the families in the Leechburg area converged at the Smiths' for Thanksgiving 2013. Johnnie bowed his head and said a prayer for the group just before the main meal. All the residents answered the prayer with "Amen" in unison.

The area now officially called itself Smithville and had just over ninety people living in it. To Kaitlin's and my surprise, she was pregnant again. I guess we had too much free time these days since living topside. At the Colonel's farm, two of the hens hatched about ten chicks each. Half of them were given to the Smiths to raise and spread the flock out further.

For the Thanksgiving festivities, the Colonel found an old tape player Pap had stashed away, as well as some retro music. The Colonel played mainly 1980s music. "I Love a Rainy Night" by Eddie Rabbit played over the speakers for the evening's first selection. With a bonfire and music echoing in the hills, the evening had a festival feel to it—something I haven't felt in years.

The group was coming together as a tight community; Smittie was elected the village's first mayor. Supplies were still going good to this point. Next summer, God willing, would require planting vegetables and growing the chicken and duck flocks even bigger and making them even more diverse. The goats the Colonel brought into the cave were not reproducing as of yet. The Colonel had hoped they would mate and produce offspring.

CHAPTER 30
December 21, 2013: Another Asteroid

"Destiny is a good thing to accept when it's going your way. When it isn't, don't call it destiny; call it injustice, treachery, or simple bad luck."

JOSEPH HELLER

Dick Ford looked down from the International Space Station to the earth's cloud cover; he had been giving amateur weather reports to Site R and NORAD based on what he saw over the last several months. It was routine now to provide observations of the weather over North America each morning. Dick would then radio it to Site R, who in turn, would advise the Colonel in Leechburg and the operations center at Wright Patterson Air Force Base and Offutt Air Force Base. The Cheyenne Mountain complex had its own direct radio contact with the space station.

Dick Ford stared out in the direction of the moon; out of the corner of his eye he caught a glimpse of something but wasn't quite sure what he saw. Dick looked back again, and then he saw it. There was an asteroid, or something like an asteroid, between the space station and the moon. His best guess was that it was about 100 miles wide. "Holy shit!" Dick exclaimed.

"What is that?" a colleague yelled back through one of the tightly crammed corridors.

"Get me Site R and NORAD—now!" Dick ordered.

****

The Colonel and Johnnie started the morning by shuttling supplies to the Smith village. There was about a foot of snow on the ground, but the Colonel had packed it down with the truck by successive trips back and forth between Smithville, Leechburg, and the cave. The Colonel had put chains on, making it easier to get through the snow. The winter was cold but not any worse than the Colonel had seen in the past.

Later that day, the Colonel and Johnnie spent their time working on a natural gas well by Smithville. After several hours of working on the well, natural gas started flowing and they then tied the houses to the gas feed. Johnnie seemed to have a skill for getting gas wells working again. Johnnie said jokingly to the Colonel, "Do you have a light?" as he connected one of the fittings to the well's nozzle.

In the spring, Johnnie thought, assuming spring came, they would probably want to bury the gas lines that now lay on top of the snow. They found several Generac generators still in the box at a hardware store in Leechburg that ran on natural gas and hoped to get them running to get the village on a small power grid, if the components had not been damaged by the EMP.

****

George Vulcanburg, the senior civilian at Wright Patterson, told Site R that they were able to tap into the power from the pod rovers. The power was some type of solar/chemical reaction that produced an adequate amount of juice relative to their size, over highly conductive wires. Heat and/or sunlight appeared to activate a sensor which in turn initiated the electrical supply. The micro-circuitry of the rover, and other equipment were more advanced that what had been invented on earth so far but, but not out of the realm of possibility to be manufactured in the future, with the equipment they already had on hand.

The plants from the pod grew at an accelerated pace but were affected negatively by the cold, going dormant only to grow again when warmth was re-applied. The plants created immense amounts of oxygen, as compared to earth plants. Several folks at Wright Patterson had now taken to eating the fruits from the bushes and reported having significant improvement in their health; all reported benefits, from more energy to increased mental clarity.

****

"Site R, this is Dick Ford at the International Space Station, we've got a lock on the other asteroid." We estimate the object is a hundred miles wide," he said as he looked out the portal at the object. "We've tracked the orbit of the object, confirming it is now in geosynchronous orbit above the equator near the center of the Atlantic Ocean—over," Dick said without leaving space for a response.

The president asked for details.

"Mr. President, we will need to reposition a satellite to get a better look at it," Dick explained. "May we have permission to make the appropriate burns to get our bird in position?"

Dick knew the president would say yes but asked just the same. He also knew doing this would up a lot of their on-board fuel. Dick was a believer in CYA (cover your ass).

"Yes, of course, Dick," President Stockwell.

"It'll take about twenty-four hours to get the bird to where we need it to be. I'll work with General Hawk at NORAD regarding the details of the burn—over," Dick said.

****

The Colonel and Johnnie were able to get the road clear past Ford Cliff and back down Route 28 to the Natrona Heights Wal-Mart. There, they loaded the truck with supplies and delivered them to the different groups of survivors they had found. Johnnie found his stash of weapons and ammo exactly where he had hidden them more than a year and half earlier.

****

"General Hawk, any new updates from NORAD in regards to the new asteroid in orbit?—over," asked the president, impatiently waiting in the Site R communications room for updates.

"We will start getting clean pictures any moment, Mr. President. We're standing by," the General replied.

The General's Intelligence officer, Captain Lawrence Butler, looked at the latest photos of the new asteroid in orbit and almost spilled his coffee when he looked at one of the close-up shots. It showed what appeared to buildings on the asteroid's surface. The asteroid also had what appeared to be thrusters on its surface.

"My goodness," the general said, as he looked at the photo the captain handed him. "How far up again?"

"The asteroid is approximately 19,000 miles above the earth in geosynchronous orbit," captain Butler replied.

General Hawk immediately passed on the information to the president.

The president said in a demanding tone, "Once the info is completely confirmed, I'd like to send a flight to Cheyenne Mountain complex to get all the information when it is ready; I'd like to go personally."

"Yes, Mr. President," the general said reluctantly.

CHAPTER 31
Spring 2014

"The day the Lord created hope was probably the same day he created Spring."
BERN WILLIAMS

The weather started warming up in March, 2014. The last snow finally melted in early April. I have now been keeping a running journal of events for over two years. Outside, plants are coming up and a few trees seem to actually be getting buds on them. Not a lot, but things are actually growing; amazingly, some plants had survived the intense heat and subsequent deep freeze. Also, some small mammals and reptiles started to emerge from their two years of hibernation. And yes, there were insects, surprisingly a lot of those survived, I noticed.

Of all the things that could have become extinct with the impacts, why not the bugs, I thought cynically to myself.

Kaitlin, the baby, and I settled back into our old home. Our house looked normal except for the plastic over the windows. Kaitlin had cleaned and decorated and it now had the smell of scented candles we used to light the rooms. Kaitlin was getting big with our second child. Everyone seemed to have their jobs amongst the family. Kaitlin and my mother watched the babies and made breakfast and dinner for everyone each day. I manned the radios, kept track of all the daily activities, and of course our inventories, keeping a log of it all. The Colonel and Johnnie helped the other families in Smithville and searched for other survivors, as well as always keeping up the search for more supplies from the various stores.

****

"General Hawk," the young airman called out across the large room in the Cheyenne Mountain complex. "Sir, it appears there is activity around the pods." The airman looked up from the satellite photo he had just analyzed. "Our latest imagery shows that plants are growing in a circle around each pod, up to a kilometer from the pod."

"What about the Russia and Africa locations, same situation, airman?" asked the general.

"I have confirmed the same thing is occurring at both those locations, too, sir. Feeling confident, he went on: "From the close-in satellite photos, sir, we can see the sphere rovers outside the pods; I assume they are planting their seeds since the weather has warmed."

****

"Site R, this is NORAD, we have a new report—over,", the general said in an authorative voice.

The president answered the call personally. "Yes, general, please proceed."

"Mr. President, we have confirmed the pods are now planting their seeds and these are growing at all three locations, Russia, Africa, and Iowa. From our tests at Wright Patterson, we have determined it takes from a couple weeks to a month for the fruit bushes to start producing their berries." He glanced down at the classified brief. "From there, they robustly grow secondary and tertiary plants from the root systems of the initial plants, as well as their seeds."

The president told General Hawk he'd planned to visit the colonel in Leechburg and then Mr. Vulcanburg, the senior civilian at the Wright Patterson AFB research facilities, the commander of Offutt AFB, and finally the Cheyenne Mountain NORAD complex, with a flyover of the pod landing sites. He added, "I plan to take an Osprey out in the next forty-eight hours, general".

All General Hawk could say was, "Roger, I understand, Mr. President, be safe."

CHAPTER 32

Coming Out of Hibernation

"No kind action ever stops with itself. One kind action leads to another."
AMELIA EARHART

The Alien Beings had searched the heavens for eons for a new world to inhabit to save their species. They set out on this journey because their home planet's sun was running out of nuclear fuel. Realizing the fate of their home planet, the Alien Beings had converted three large asteroids into arks of a sort and sent their species into three different directions to find new planets to inhabit. The asteroid ships used a propulsion system that achieved a speed just under one-hundredth the speed of light.

The plan was for at least one, and hopefully all three asteroid ships to find other habitable planets. The trip to the planet the Alien Beings now orbited had taken just over 3,200 earth years to reach. A smaller craft, much faster, set out in front of the main asteroid ship and found earth about 400 years earlier, as it scouted ahead of the main ship. The scout ship first visited Europe, then North America, hovering over an Indian village near modern day Kittanning, Pennsylvania, in the seventeenth century. The Alien Beings abducted humans from both Europe and North America and then returned them after they performed medical tests on them.

The radio reports the Alien Beings received over 2,200 years ago gave accounts of the final days of their home planet. Most of their species chose not to reproduce in the waning years of their homeland, thus the loss of life on their home planet was minimal. The last of the Alien Beings on the home planet reported how the oceans had evaporated as their sun expanded to many times its normal size. Then one day, the radio reports just stopped coming. Now, the three arks were all that was left of the Alien Being species. The light from the star's explosion was seen about the time of the birth of Christ; the exploding stars was even visible during daylight.

The covenant amongst the Alien Beings was actually very altruistic; their species collectively agreed to find a new planet devoid of any intelligent life to re-establish their way of life. They decided that they would not affect any planet that had intelligent life, even at the cost of their own species going extinct. Earlier in their journey, the Alien Beings came across a habitable planet, only about 500 years into their trip, but passed it by when intelligent life was found.

Having received radio reports from the other two asteroid ships that they had found no habitable worlds, the Alien Being overseers of the earth-bound asteroid ship knew they had no choice but to give up their moral position if they were to save their species; so they chose to forget the covenant they had agreed to so long ago. Eons in space, and the loss of their home world had hardened their hearts. They hatched a plot to divert two asteroids from the asteroid belt between Mars and Jupiter and send them on a collision course with earth to eliminate the indigenous intelligent life and assume control of the planet.

The advance Alien Being team set the plot into action shortly after their initial visit to earth 400 years ago. The two asteroids were set to hit the earth just prior to the arrival of the Alien Being main asteroid ship. The calculations were made to have the asteroids hit where they did—the Pacific and Atlantic oceans—to optimize the destruction of the indigenous populations but allow for a quick reconstitution of the planet's ecosystem. And of course, the plan was to keep this plan secret to the general Alien Being population. After their first visit to earth, on the way out of the solar system, the Alien Beings attached thrusters on two asteroids that started making subtle course corrections for their plan.

Four hundred years ago, the people of earth rode horses and used mainly bows and arrows, having only rudimentary firearms. In between the Alien Beings' initial visit 400 years ago and the present, the faster ship came back to earth several times to check up on their new home. The indigenous life had amazed the Alien Beings—how fast they had progressed technologically!

The Alien Beings became concerned when they witnessed the humans detonating atomic weapons. They went so far as to hover over several United States and Soviet Union missile silos and fry all the electronics several years later. The human leadership perceived these actions taken by the Alien Beings as altruistic in nature, kicking off peace talks and the SALT agreements. The Alien Being observations were kept secret from the general population by both superpowers. However, in the end these actions were only part of the Alien Beings' plan to protect their new home.

What also concerned the Alien Beings was watching the human's fledgling space program blossom. The aliens witnessed several moon landings and hovered around various spacecraft in orbit. At one point, the Alien Being scout ship went so far to fire a particle-beam weapon at one of the humans' space ships to slow down their space programs.

In the three decades prior to the arrival of the main asteroid ship, earth's air defense systems had improved so much that the advance ship could not even enter the atmosphere without risking fire from human aircraft. The humans' technological progress was remarkable by comparison to their own; the overseers realized that the humans would surpass their technology within a few more centuries if they continued at their current pace.

*****

Once the process to re-animate the Alien Beings started, it could not be reversed. The leader of the Alien Beings gave the order to start the reactors for the extra power required for the reanimation process. The process would take about two earth months to complete. The pods on the planet's surface appeared to be carrying out their mission of growing edible plants for the soon-to-come Alien Being population. The pods at the Iowa location were the most successful. The climate on the planet's surface was now warming and stabilizing, as the Alien Beings had known it would. The reanimated Alien Beings would need sustenance and shelter in short order, and these the asteroid ship itself could not provide.

The small contingency of "awake" Alien Beings started the checklist to reanimate the two million or so Alien Beings from deep suspended animation. The main body of "asleep" Alien Beings had been in a frozen state for many more years than they were supposed to be. By virtue of how long they were frozen in suspended animation, the Alien Beings overseers' computer model simulations estimated only about half of their species would survive the reanimation process.

Once reanimated, the million plus Alien Beings could not survive on the asteroid for more than a couple weeks at best, with the craft's limited resources for a population of that size. Another consideration was the estimated million Alien Beings that would not survive reanimation process; these dead bodies would pose a serious health risk to those Alien Beings still living.

Smittie, the leader of Smithville, started getting the gardens in the ground. Smittie worked with his family as well as other members of the village to get almost three acres of ground tilled and planted. Other folks in Smithville started organizing canning supplies and researching various food storage techniques. The village also worked to expand their flock of chickens. Four of the hens they received as chicks last year now sat on their own nests, as well as one of the female Pekin ducks. The chickens and ducks had found a new food source above ground too—insects. For now, the food supplies left over from the pre-impact days were still plentiful; this would not be the case forever, and they all knew it.

The Smithville village had grown further, with four new clusters of survivors from the Gibsonia area found by the Colonel and Johnnie. The village even boasted electricity and running water now, and all the houses had their own wells. Each family also had a working car. Smithville looked like something out of the 1950s, with all the old cars in the driveways and laundry hung on clotheslines.

Eventually, the almost endless supply of gasoline would break down and not be usable. The Colonel was already planning for this contingency by having one of the mechanics work on several newer flex fuel vehicles that could run on both gas and alcohol. The mechanics had to get past the damaged electronic parts destroyed in the EMP pulse on the day of the impacts.

The group celebrated the Fourth of July 2014 at Smithville. The fledging town used a pavilion from Lingrow Farm for the celebration. Smittie fashioned tiki torches around the celebrations area and music played over old crackly speakers. The event featured fresh vegetables and several roasted chickens.

Smithville now had over forty chickens, mainly chicks, from the hens' previous efforts. The Colonel had given twenty chicks each from his flock to Site R, Ohio, and NORAD when an Osprey came through the previous month. During the stop, the Colonel accompanied the president to Ohio, Nebraska, and Colorado.

CHAPTER 33

Invasion: August 27, 2014

"Destruction cometh; and they shall seek peace, and there shall be none."

EZEKIEL 7:25 / OLD TESTAMENT

The Alien Beings awoke virtually every minute now from their 3,200 year suspended animation. To the Alien Beings that just awoke, it only seemed like a month since they left their home planet. The electronic vibrations sent to stimulate their muscles had them in decent physical shape, but they still felt groggy as they stepped out of the cocoon-like vestibule they used for their deep sleep. It was apparent the Alien Beings could not re-animate about a third of their "frozen" population, but this number was actually higher than the overseers had originally projected. Surprisingly, 1.3 million of their species had survived the reanimation process.

The re-animated Alien Beings wandered around on the asteroid ship trying to find out who had survived and who had not. Emotions ran deep at the discovery of the loss of a friend or loved one and the realization that their entire world was now gone. The process of getting on the asteroid spaceships had been its own challenge so many years ago, with only a small number of the species being selected by the lottery system. Even then, the risks were high and required accepting waking up with everything they had ever known long gone.

The plan by the overseers was to set up three separate colonies on earth. Two smaller colonies, one in Africa and one in Asia), would be set up with approximately 300,000 Alien Beings each, and one large colony in North America with the remaining 700,000 Alien Beings. Due to the pre-positioned pods having the best results growing sustenance at the North American location, this area was selected by the Alien Being overseers to get the lion's share of the asteroid's population.

The Alien Beings communicated through telepathy and had an electronic computer implant to allow one-way mass media communications. The Alien Beings could also communicate telepathically without the aid of a transmitter, but this type of communication could only occur in close proximity to another Alien Being. The attenuation of the interpersonal Alien Being communications was about the same as a human conversation's audible range. The kind of messages received via the computer implants was a mass communications medium of sorts from the Alien Being overseers.

As the Alien Beings awoke, they received communications through these implants that a suitable world had been found. However, the world they found had suffered an unfortunate meteor strike that had killed practically all indigenous life several years prior to their arrival.

The Alien Being landing ships offered a one-way trip to their new world from the mother ship. Each of the landing ships was supplied with such necessities as shelters, vehicles, clothing, power generation equipment, and food prepared and packaged by manufacturers long since dead. Though the Alien Beings loaded a small contingent of weapons along with their supplies, the plan was never to take any planet by force from any fellow intelligent beings.

The three landing locations on their new planet loosely matched the geographic groups the Alien Beings had on their home planet. Over the years in space travel, the overseers had taken turns staying animated and would now serve as the leaders to each location on their new planet's surface. The overseers stood out from the masses of Alien Beings, appearing much older.

The main landing ships had a distinctive V shape, and each ship carried about 30,000 Alien Beings. The ships themselves would also serve as a temporary shelter and administrative building once on the ground for some of the Alien Beings.

The landing crafts departed from the asteroid at thirty-six-minute intervals and made long contrails as they punched through earth's thick atmosphere. The journey to the new world would take about a day and a half. With a third of the Alien Beings dead, the landing ships were less crowded for the trip to the planet's surface.

****

The International Space Station's orbit took it over the Atlantic Ocean. Astronaut Dick Ford saw the contrails from what appeared to be large meteors. One of the contrails tracked to the location in Iowa. Dick called Site R and reported his observation. Site R acknowledged the transmission and Dick Ford and crew were advised to maintain radio silence from this point forward unless it was an absolute emergency. In turn, Site R advised the Cheyenne Mountain complex, who started work observing this new activity.

Site R had advised NORAD from this point on to have a team go a hundred miles away from the Cheyenne Mountain complex twenty-four hours from now and radio its reports to a person who would do the same at Site R; the radio transmissions would be brief, and to the point.

****

The Colonel was advised that there would be radio silence with Site R from this point until further notice. He wasn't told why, but he could speculate after having talked with the president on the way to Colorado Springs a month back. The Colonel and Johnnie had already started gathering and organizing assorted weaponry and ammo from the various National Guard armories in the area.

****

From the spy satellite images, the intel officer at the Cheyenne Mountain complex was easily able to see the alien landing crafts that had landed at the three locations. The landing craft now intermixed within the foliage the aliens had pre-positioned with the pods they sent down a year earlier. With the spy telescopes' sensitive magnification, the intel captain could see the individual Alien Beings walking around the landing crafts. They were gray bipedal with arms, legs, and large heads; they wore some type of outer garments.

From what the captain could tell, the Alien Beings appeared very similar to the gray skinned alien's with big heads and long skinny arms and legs he'd seen in various UFO movies he had watched on TV over the years; he suspected these aliens had visited the earth for years. The similarities seemed too coincidental.

Each landing craft appeared to unload pre-fabricated buildings. There also appeared truck-like wheeled vehicles moving supplies. The buildings appeared to be set up in communities distributed around the landing crafts.

General Hawk loaded all the intelligence he had gathered into two packages being too large to transmit via radio, as he and the president had planned. In turn, a convoy of three vehicles departed Colorado Springs north towards Denver, then across Nebraska and northern Iowa. The convoy did not stop except to refuel before reaching Wright Patterson in Dayton. The team had practiced this trip several times over the last month, clearing the roads in advance. With all burnable debris already gone, the roads were relatively clear on the route from Colorado to Ohio. The NORAD team used a deuce and a half fitted with a snowplow to push any dead vehicles off the roadways. Attached to each courier package was an incendiary grenade in case of the worse-case scenario of capture.

When the courier team arrived at Wright Patterson, an Osprey took off within five minutes, never going above 1,000 feet above the surface landing at Site R; a crew standing by immediately shuttled the Osprey into its hanger as the intelligence package it carried was rushed into the site for analysis.

****

The Alien Being completed their landings in about two and a half days; the methodology for those waiting to leave the asteroid seemed haphazard, with the procession of landing craft going in fits and starts. The landing zones at the three locations had turned into virtual cities overnight, filling with new occupants. From the spy satellite, it was clear that the Alien Beings had now cultivated additional land; these areas were sown with alien seeds using the odd-looking tractors. Judging by the fencing going up, it appeared areas were also set aside for farming and possibly some type of alien livestock.

The Alien Beings set up their housing along previous human made roadways. The spy satellites also showed that each Alien Being landing site had a defensive perimeter set up around it, with apparent security positioned at what were once previous road intersections in a circular grid approximately fifty kilometers in all directions around the main landing crafts.

The spy satellite revealed that these security forces appeared to be minimal at best, with about a squad-sizes contingent of

Alien Beings; there were approximately twelve Alien Beings on duty at any given time at each of the various checkpoints. The intel team wondered if the guards were in place to keep the aliens from leaving as opposed to keeping invaders from entering.

The main asteroid ship showed no new activity after about ten days from the last landing ship making its re-entry into the earth's atmosphere. The Alien Beings appeared to have one flying craft at each location on top of one of the larger landing crafts. The best estimation was that the flying craft was the size of a large passenger jet. The various landing craft at the three sites had not moved since the invasion started. The intel team assumed that the landing craft with the smaller craft on top housed the Alien Being leadership.

CHAPTER 34

Abduction

"It is wiser to find out than to suppose."
ALBERT EINSTEIN

The analysts at NORAD inside the Cheyenne Mountain complex started a campaign to identify and track any radio transmissions emitted from the three Alien Being landing locations. They also had tried to obtain signal intelligence from the asteroid ship, but without success. The analyst finally identified a signal source in one of the lower radio frequency bands coming from the Iowa landing zone. The signal had a consistency similar to human digital communications as opposed to an analog voice signal, which was what they had anticipated. The radio signals were complex but seemed to be binary in form. A team of computer scientists worked day and night trying to decipher and understand the signals.

Human intelligence was a misnomer in this particular case. It was decided additional intelligence was needed on the Alien Beings themselves. It was also decided that kidnapping one or more Alien Beings would have great intelligence value, and so an abduction plan was devised.

With absolute radio silence, a courier left Wright Patterson and drove across the wastelands of the Midwest with a message from Site R for Colorado Springs and NORAD via Offutt AFB. The message satchel contained the details of the Alien Being abduction plan to General Hawk and NORAD, from the national security advisor, Chip, and President Stockwell. At the same time, a courier left from Colorado Springs for Wright Patterson and then Site R, acknowledging the plan and giving the leader at Wright Patterson a heads-up of another mission coming its way.

The process of refining the plan went on for several days, with correspondence and intelligence exchanged amongst the sites. West of Ohio, the landscape was barren of any combustible debris from the firestorm. Due to the roadways still being cluttered with debris east of Dayton, the hops between Wright Patterson, Leechburg, and Site R were accomplished via Osprey.

Finally, the actual plan to abduct an Alien Being was formalized among the various locations; it took five days and countless miles by the couriers to codify the actual plan. The abduction plan had various moving parts, both to mitigate risk and protect the human enclaves.

****

The abduction team assembled near Offutt AFB in Council Bluffs, Iowa. There, the team had gathered multiple specialized vehicles, plus extra fuel. The Alien Being transport vehicle was set up to isolate and separate any captured Alien Beings. The Alien Being transport vehicle—a military box van—also had lead around the holding cages to dampen potential radio distress calls from the captured Alien Beings.

****

Intelligence from the spy satellite showed two Alien Beings well outside their security perimeter trying to set up a small farm in central Iowa near the town of Oxford Junction. This Alien Being couple appeared to have had great success growing their alien plant life and seemed to be loners. The couple almost seemed to be hiding from the collective in the main landing area.

The Alien Being couple was found totally by accident, as the various couriers noticed the alien plant life north of I-80 on their courier runs. How the Alien Beings did not cross paths with the constant procession of couriers surprised everyone.

The Alien Being abduction team would attempt to capture the aliens by tranquilizing them and then transport them to St. Louis, Missouri, where a second team waited to bring them the rest of the way to Wright Patterson. A team of scientists was on standby in Ohio to examine the Alien Beings, and any accompanying technology captured, as soon as it arrived.

The scientists had by now reverse-engineered the power source and circuitry from the pod and rovers. Except for the chemical compounds used to make the electricity, and the fact that the circuitry and its connectivity was very low voltage, using very highly conductive material, most of the pod's equipment had minimal intelligence value.

****

Army Special Forces Major Richard Paine commanded the retrieval team. Major Paine had about twenty personnel under his command on the abduction team, including drivers and security. Wearing ghillie suits, five members of the abduction team crept up to within half a kilometer of the Alien Being farmstead. From what they could see, the two Alien Beings appeared to be about four feet tall, thin, and were quite fragile looking—and, most importantly, they were alone.

The Alien Beings used hand tools similar to hoes and shovels to plant their fields. For their living space, they had a tent-like structure. The close-in team observed them for approximately twenty-four hours to ensure they were the only two occupants of the farmstead.

The Alien Beings went into the tent structure at dark, apparently to rest or sleep, and emerged again at about seven a.m. the next morning; they were apparently not nocturnal.

Major Paine decided the retrieval team would abduct the Alien Beings when they were away from their tent structures to mitigate the risk of any distress calls or beacons being activated. Ideally, the retrieval team would take the Alien Beings from the field they were working and immediately separate them and drug them. A second team would then load up all equipment in and around the tent area in two vehicles.

Major Paine maneuvered his team within 100 meters of their targets. Two snipers crawled to within range of their targets with the tranquilizer dart guns. Each Alien Being was hit in an exposed fleshy area of their upper arm, simultaneously. The darts appeared to have no effect; the Alien Beings pulled the darts from their arms, looking quizzical. The teams then literally jumped the Alien Beings and duct-taped their extremities together. While in close proximity of the Alien Beings, Paine sensed they were somehow trying to communicate with him telepathically; he also sensed great fear in the Alien Beings' minds. With a swift hit from the butt of an M16 rifle to the head of each Alien Being, they were knocked unconscious and the telepathic sensation immediately stopped.

****

The drive team had the Alien Beings in the box van and wheels turning in less than five minutes after they were captured. The guards in the back were warned about the telepathic communications and told to hit the Alien Beings in the head again if they awoke. However, the security team was not to overdo it, either, whatever that meant. The second team loaded up all the Alien Being equipment in the other vehicles. The deuce and a halves were on the road, wheels turning, in less twenty minutes after the abduction. After the equipment team finished their work, the area where the Alien Beings had lived looked like no one had ever lived there.

****

The drive across the Midwest was nerve-racking for everyone on the abduction team. Major Paine kept looking skyward for the captured Alien Beings' brethren to swoop down and rescue them, ray guns blasting; but that did not occur. The team was put on edge with the thunderous blast of a close lightning strike. The relief team in St. Louis took over driving the vehicles. The relief team refueled the vehicles and drove on to their final destination at Wright Patterson AFB.

In Ohio, the reception team waited at the loading docks for the new arrivals. The waiting scientist had already set up separate locations for each of the Alien Beings within the underground complex at the base. The complex already had facilities in place to accommodate these types of arrivals—sort of. In the old days, the NSA agents hustled freaks of nature into the facility late at night in U-Hauls, as well as other non-descript vehicles, for study.

When the deuce and a halves with the alien equipment arrived twelve hours later, the reception team took the aliens' various accoutrements to one of the deepest parts of the complex, in case any radio distress beacons on the equipment were to become activated. A single microphone keying from a location over a hundred miles away, from a special courier on behalf of Wright Patterson to Site R radio, signaled the mission was a success.

****

The equipment team inventoried all the alien equipment found at the abduction site. The tent was just that—a tent. Its contents included two cot-like beds, chairs, a table, clothing, a device similar to E-book reader, seeds, food, and water containers with water inside them. Surprisingly, the Alien Being couple had no weapons. The E-book, as everyone referred to it now, seemed to activate when held. Its interface seemed to work by telepathic abilities, creating three-dimensional mind pictures. The best anyone could tell, it was not an outbound radio transmitter or distress beacon. It did receive inputs, though, and relay them telepathically, but they were as yet unintelligible. By the spartan way the camp was set up, it seemed the abducted Alien Beings were sort of rebels within their own species and just trying to hide.

****

The Alien Beings were X-rayed, weighed, measured, photographed, and tapped for fluid samples. They were about four feet tall and not overly muscular. They appeared to breathe oxygen. They had large heads, black eyes with no iris, small mouths and small, nubby teeth. Their skin was gray and leathery. Their blood was a grayish-blue color and seemed to circulate oxygen throughout the body, as well as caloric energy from food. The scientists guessed that the Alien Beings were asexual, or possibly female with the ability to generate self-fertilized eggs to reproduce. The X-rays showed a bone structure, a digestive system, and heart-based circulatory structure. The Alien Beings actually looked like all the stereotyped gray beings used in all the movies.

Judging from the X-rays, both Alien Beings had what appeared to be electronic devices implanted directly into their brains. The micro-circuitry appeared similar to the pod circuitry. It apparently ran off the natural electricity produced by their bodies.

The medical team was now waiting for the Alien Beings to regain consciousness. A staff psychologist, a linguist, and an intelligence officer all stood by to observe the Alien Beings upon their awakening. The intelligence team set up separate cells with food, water, and cots taken from the abduction site. It was agreed to move the Alien Beings to pre-arranged holding cells when it appeared they were about to wake up.

Each abducted Alien Being had, in addition to the scientific staff, two guards on duty watching over it at all times. The inner guard was instructed to shoot the Alien Being immediately if it appeared that it was trying to manipulate the scientific staff to facilitate its escape or to harm any of the staff. In case things went totally awry, the outer guard had a box with a button that could blow the entire corridor. Under no circumstances were the Alien Beings to escape from the underground facility.

About twenty-four hours after their abduction, one of the Alien Beings started coming to. The intelligence team had been waiting for this moment.

CHAPTER 35
Lay of the Land

"If a man's mind becomes pure, his surroundings will also become pure."
BUDDHA

The Colonel and Johnnie had kept up their survey of western Pennsylvania and even ventured into eastern Ohio and northern West Virginia to look for survivors. On their trips they found a family or an enclave of survivors in approximately every other town. Their surveys took them out in about a 150-mile radius from Leechburg. The debris-cluttered roadways made travel slow and difficult.

More folks survived to the east, and less to the west towards Ohio, which made sense. The Colonel came across an enclave of eighty-two Virginia Military Institute cadets, plus other survivors, in Elkins, West Virginia. The cadet leader said that there were over 800 cadets still alive spread out in all directions from around Lexington, Virginia.

The count was now over 1,800 survivors that the Colonel and Johnnie had visually confirmed. If the cadet's story was verified, there were another 700 more Virginia Military Institute cadets alive to add to the population. The Colonel, being an alumnus of the Institute, beamed with the news of the Virginia Military Institute cadets.

The Colonel and Johnnie enlisted folks in the periphery to extend the surveys outwards even further; they also encouraged folks to double up in towns and even to consider consolidating into towns similar to Smithville, for mutual support.

The Colonel and Johnnie took note of folks that had military backgrounds and combat experience. They also noted policemen and people with medical experience as well as other useful skills that might be required in a post-impact world.

****

Site R had its own active survey team, and they started surveying out from their location near Harrisburg for survivors. They had approximately the same results, right up to the high-water mark of the tsunami on the Atlantic seaboard. From the high watermark and east, there were no survivors. The total devastation had made this land almost uninhabitable.

One enclave of survivors, approximately 75 men and women, discovered by the Site R survey team, had taken up fishing for sustenance; they caught mainly catfish and carp that had survived in the deep pools of the Susquehanna River near Harrisburg, Pennsylvania.

This enclave had survived the heat wave by taking shelter in the Kittanning Tunnel on the Pennsylvania Turnpike when their cars died. This group made its way to Harrisburg looking for relief and took shelter in an upscale housing development when things turned cold, riding out the extended winter in a series of houses connected by a tunnel system. A young social worker kept the group together as their leader during this time; she had exhibited leadership that belied her age.

The Site R survey team discovered a majority of the Virginia Military Institute Corps of Cadets survived while running into an enclave of cadet and survivors in Winchester, Virginia. In Winchester, the cadets related the same story to the Site R survey team as the cadets found in Elkins. The cadet leader said that the corps of cadets split up by company and dispersed to various locations in central Virginia, stretching into the east side of West Virginia. The cadet leader said each of the enclaves had taken care of the other survivors they had found along the way.

CHAPTER 36
Homeward Bound

"Life is either a daring adventure or nothing."
HELEN KELLER

A short message came from the International Space Station to Site R and NORAD. Dick Ford radioed, "Our oxygen supply has diminished and we will soon need to take the emergency escape pod back to earth."

It was agreed that Larry "Buck" Rogers, one of Ford's astronaut counterparts, would stay on board. The medical doctor diagnosed Buck with terminal cancer caused by exposure to the cosmic radiation in space. According to the doc, the cancer would kill Buck long before the remaining oxygen, and other supplies required by one person would run out on the space station. Buck would maintain an eye in the sky for another two to four months, depending on how fast it took the cancer in his body to metastasize. Ford readied the remaining supplies, along with pain medicine and a special drug "cocktail" the doc made that would take care of Buck's final pains. Buck wore this vial of medicine on a necklace.

The rest of the team would eject from the escape pod the next day over North America, pass through the atmosphere, and land in upstate New York, near Niagara Falls. Ford and the other surviving astronauts would then make their way over land to Site R. Along the way, they were to survey the towns, taking a census of the survivors. The astronauts would also take inventory of pre-impact supplies and secure the several National Guard armories they encountered en route.

Looking out of the small windows on top of the capsule, the astronauts saw the contrails streaking away from the escape pod as it fell through the atmosphere. All felt a relief when the parachute rockets fired and the escape pod slowed down with a jolt. The airbag system fired as designed when the escape pod got within 100 feet of the ground. The landing was uneventful, albeit with a harder than anticipated touchdown.

With their bodies weakened from living in a zero-gravity atmosphere, plus a very low calorie diet, the astronauts found it hard to acclimate to terra firma right away. The astronauts easily found supplies in Niagara Falls but found only a handful of survivors in the area. They actually heard Niagara Falls in the distance. However, the astronauts did not make the effort to walk over to see it.

****

The two Alien Beings started to wake up, as intelligence officers stood by their bedsides, anticipating the moment. The first Alien Being woke up startled. It attempted to break free from the bed; the restraints were overkill to the Alien Being's actual strength. However, the intel officer took no chances by undoing them.

The officer made eye contact with the Alien Being, then she offered water to it, which it readily drank through a straw from a container found at the abduction site in Iowa. All of a sudden, the intel officer saw the Alien Being's thoughts. At first, it was a mishmash of images, like an old television going in and out of stations, or a silent movie, only in color versus black and white.

The best the officer could tell from these sketchy communications was that the Alien Being was scared and hungry; it did not appear to be hostile, however. As a gesture of trust, the intel officer had the arm restraints removed. Then, the officer let the Alien Being eat some of the food that was in its tent and drink more water. After eating and drinking, the Alien Being appeared to zone in and out, and then lost consciousness again. The arm restraints were left off, but the leg restraints were kept in place. The Alien Being slept for another seven hours.

The second Alien Being awoke several hours later making the most hideous screaming noise, everyone in the room jumped backwards, the guard took aim, the second Alien Being then went unconscious apparently from hyperventilating. The Alien Beings went in and out consciousness several times, staying awake longer each time. In general, they seemed lethargic in their current situation. The lead doctor worried the Alien Beings may have been hit too hard in the head during the abduction, possibly causing brain damage.

****

In the weeks' and month after the invasion, the satellite imagery from NORAD showed the Alien Being clusters around the large landing crafts had become bustling cities, with lighted streets. Between the cities there was increased plant life and crop activity. The Alien Beings appeared to even use the shells, mainly burned-out basements of former houses, for shelter around their landing sites and their emerging cities.

CHAPTER 37

The Jig is Up

"Change is hard because people overestimate the value of what they have—and underestimate the value of what they may gain by giving that up."
JAMES BELASCO AND RALPH STAYER

The spy team at NORAD kept a close eye on the area around the abduction site in Oxford Junction, Iowa, from the time the abduction team took the two Alien Beings to Wright Patterson. Satellite photos showed the alien retrieval site in Iowa remained undisturbed for more than three weeks. Then, the close-up run of photos from the day previous showed a group of Alien Beings camped out near the loners' site. In the successive passes of the spy satellite, photos showed Alien Beings at the site, apparently searching for the two missing Alien Beings.

General Hawk tasked a team of two soldiers to pass this information on to Wright Patterson and Site R. The courier team would have to hand-deliver the additional intel; it would be too long to transmit via radio and could not include the intelligence photographs. In the event of capture, General Hawk instructed the soldiers to destroy the message satchel with a white phosphorous grenade and encouraged (but did not order) the courier team to commit suicide before they could be questioned, lest they give out intelligence about the human military and leadership capabilities to the Alien Beings. This was a rough mission for any soldier to volunteer for. But, there was no shortage of volunteers.

As the couriers got under way from Colorado Springs with the abduction site intelligence reports and photos, a radio team for NORAD in Colorado went out to their random location one hundred miles from Colorado Springs for a short routine radio transmission to the corresponding Site R team also a hundred miles from the Site R location. They both set up and transmitted at their prescribed time. The short coded transmission was less than ninety seconds in length. Both radio teams immediately broke down their respective gear and were already five miles from their transmission locations when first the Colorado transmit location, and then Pennsylvania radio location were pulverized by some force within five minutes apart.

Even five miles away, debris came raining down on the Colorado radio team; the driver nearly lost control of his vehicle in the confusion. The Pennsylvania team was further away from the explosion and ten minutes from its transmission site, but still felt the concussion. By luck, both teams got away unhurt, but it was now clear that the jig was up with the Alien Beings. There would have to be complete radio silence from this point forward. This meant additional road couriers back and forth between the locations, which had its own inherent set of risks.

****

When word got to the president about the attack on the Site R radio team, he immediately issued the order to formalize complete radio silence, including the brief messages they had been transmitting and any other radio transmission, including CB transmissions, which had become a popular means of communicating amongst the survivor enclaves. The president then sent couriers calling for General Hawk from NORAD, the commander at Offutt AFB, the senior civilian, Mr. Vulcanburg from Wright Patterson, Commander Bagley from the remaining nuclear submarine, the VMI Regimental Commander Van Price and Gunny Sergeant Joyce, and Colonel Robert Steele from Leechburg to meet with him in two weeks at a yet to be determined location in western Pennsylvania. The subject of the meeting was to discuss possible plans of action to deal with earth's uninvited guests.

This effort would be difficult to facilitate with complete radio silence. President Stockwell ordered the Osprey aircraft at Site R dispersed to other locations further away from the site. He also formed a second leadership team, with an appointed vice president to take charge in the event Site R was destroyed. The nuclear submarine was ordered to take out all three locations in two months if Captain Bagley did not return from the leadership conference.

The president realized that in light of the attacks on the radio teams, Site R was now vulnerable. He appointed Chip Colby to stand as acting vice president. Without any pomp and circumstance, Chip was sworn in by a military JAG officer on a King James Bible at the Site R facility, and then he and his team of advisors were quickly scooted away to another location. The location the vice president and his leadership team decided upon was the Greenbriar Hotel Bunker in West Virginia. The President charged the company of Virginia Military Institute cadets that had taken residence at the hotel to provide security for the vice president and his staff.

****

The Colonel got the word in Leechburg to cease all radio communications. He immediately dispatched couriers of his own to pass the word to every enclave of survivors he administrated in western Pennsylvania, eastern Ohio, and northern West Virginia to cease all radio communications. The Colonel doubted the

Alien Beings could detect the weak CB signals, but he did not want to take any chances and complied fully and immediately with the presidential order. The Colonel gave no rationale for his order of radio silence to his territories, but he felt sure that folks would adhere to it.

To this point, the majority of the survivors were unaware of the Alien Beings on the three continents, and they had been kept in the dark mainly out of their leaders' fear of panic breaking out in a world that had already gone mad. The Colonel first found out about the Alien Beings when he shared an Osprey flight to NORAD with the president a few months earlier. The Colonel then briefed Johnnie, Kevin, and me, but even our wives were not to know this information.

The president had tasked the key survivor leaders to start identifying combat-ready troops to call upon, if needed; he wanted a current update from his enclave leaders before the leadership conference in two weeks. The Colonel and Johnnie started making the rounds of the survivors as I coordinated these efforts and generated reports for the meeting called by the president.

****

Just days before the meeting in western Pennsylvania, the Colonel informed certain people under his charge of the Alien Being situation. He met with his enclave leaders and briefed them, then asked them to brief the respective folks in their charge. The Colonel also tasked each enclave to institute a 24/7 security detail as well as to start mobilizing combat-able men and women and their accompanying weaponry. The Colonel asked for troop strength reports from the enclaves in thirty-six hours, with contingents of troops ready to fully mobilize within seventy-two hours. The Colonel said he would soon provide a rally point for the troops to meet.

Both the intel officers and scientists at Wright Patterson had worked with the abducted Alien Beings to obtain intelligence. They had found someone who mastered communicating with the Alien Beings. From visual conversations with the human translator, the lead intel officer determined the earth's uninvited guests originally came from a dying, and now dead, planet about thirty-two light years away.

The Alien Beings from the dying planet had created three ships crafted out of asteroids, sort of like arks, containing representations of their civilization that deployed in three different directions. Even with the asteroids' vast resources, they were still required to put most of the Alien Beings in a state of suspended animation for the journey. The asteroid space ships' propulsion could only achieve about one-one hundredth the speed of light, the interpreter determined from the abducted Alien Beings' telepathy.

The interpreter said that the Alien Beings had been told by their leadership when they were awakened that they found this planet, earth, already in the state it was in now. From the perspective of the abducted Alien Beings, the trip to our planet only seemed like a couple months instead of thousands of years. The last memories the Alien Beings had were leaving their planet and their families. Most of those who awoke were in total shock from losing almost a third of their loved ones—those who could not be reanimated—along with the realization their world, and all they ever knew, was now gone.

The intel officers interrogated the Alien Beings regarding weapons their species may have brought with them. For the most part, from what the interrogator could ascertain, it appeared that the Alien Beings were peaceful. They apparently possessed only minimal weaponry, mainly used for hunting, and of course their asteroid ship had a particle beam to displace debris that was in front of it as it traveled through space. The particle beam was what most likely fired at the mobile radio transmission teams a couple weeks before. The intel officer could sense a sadness from the Alien Beings losing their world. She could also sense the Alien Beings sensed her own sadness and anger at the destruction of the Earth. To that, the Alien Beings had a feeling of shame. However, no one could tell for sure if the abductees were being truthful or concealing what they knew about their leadership's true intentions.

CHAPTER 38
By a Hair

"The world is getting to be such a dangerous place, a man is lucky to get out of it alive."
W. C. FIELDS

Four days later, General Hawk in Colorado Springs got the word to attend the president's leadership call from an inbound courier from Wright Patterson AFB. The message read, "General Hawk is to meet in Leechburg, Pennsylvania, for a leadership conference in 10 days.".

General Hawk asked his aide, "Where in the hell is Leechburg, Pennsylvania?"

His aide just shrugged his shoulders and said, "I don't know, sir. Never heard of it."

The trip east to Leechburg would take about thirty hours of non-stop driving, assuming no issues cropped up along the way. The general loaded up his small convoy of four vehicles for the cross-country trek through the burned-out wastelands.

The general rode in a classic red 1965 Ford Mustang. Three older Jimmies contained a security detail and several of the general's various aides. All in the group knew that the convoy had to keep radio silence. The trip would take them north out of Colorado, through Nebraska, skirt around northern Iowa, then along the Great Lakes and finally south to western Pennsylvania, stopping at Wright Patterson briefly to get a firsthand intelligence brief from the base's scientists regarding the abducted Alien Beings and their technology. General Hawk was also curious as to what the Alien Beings looked like.

The plan was for General Hawk to head out at 7 a.m., four days out from the leadership conference, to traverse the danger area around Iowa during daylight hours.

The first twelve hours of the drive were completely uneventful. The general was finally able to take in the total extent of the damage caused from the impact's firestorm; he used a digital camera that survived the EMP pulse inside the Cheyenne Mountain complex to document the landscape. However, a lot of the photos were blurry, taken on the move with the convoy just stopping long enough to refuel using jerry cans and team biological breaks.

Hour after hour of driving through the charred wastelands of Colorado and Nebraska revealed no signs of indigenous life, neither plant nor animal. The general finally did see Alien Being plant life that had spread into northern Iowa. The growth's bluish-green hue contrasted with the surrounding charred landscape. Unfortunately, the cultivators of these plants also saw the general's convoy zoom by them as they worked in the fields.

****

General Hawk was going over some of his reports in the passenger seat with his executive officer Keith Stanley, who was driving, when a loud concussion came up from the rear of the vehicle. The general looked back in time to see debris from the particle weapon pouring down on top of the convoy. The convoy sped up as fast as they could safely. Five minutes later, a second concussion hit; it was much closer, about five miles back this time. The general's executive officer almost lost control of the

Mustang from the debris that came down in front of him. He had to maneuver around some of the larger pieces of debris.

The leader of the security detail pointed to the executive officer to take a side road south, as the three security vehicles kept on the same track. Keith's Mustang sped off to the side, while the three security vehicles kept speeding down the same road. About five minutes later another explosion struck from the particle beam.

****

The Colonel and Johnnie had a good day. On their way back from West Virginia, they came upon an enclave of survivors now living in Mount Lebanon, outside of Pittsburgh. The group initially lived in the Liberty and Fort Pitt tunnels and moved to Mount Lebanon to build a survival camp. The leader of the group was a prominent member of the Pittsburgh Steelers caught by sheer happenstance in the Fort Pitt tunnel. The Colonel finally advised the group of the Alien Beings; Johnnie asked for volunteers to participate in a strike on the Alien Being city. Everyone in the group raised their hand to volunteer. One of the members was an elderly woman who used a walker.

****

The most recent explosion was closer to the three Jimmies. It appeared their plan was working: the Alien Beings' fire was being drawn away from the general. At this point, all three vehicles went in separate directions. One vehicle drove back through the shot-up roadway, surviving by hiding in a tunnel. Another Jimmy drove about thirty-five miles north and parked under a large bridge. With the Alien Beings' particle beam finally closing the gap, the final Jimmy, which had continued speeding in the original direction of travel, finally fell victim to a blast about twenty-five minutes later.

It appeared that the Alien Being particle beam took about five minutes to recharge before it could be fired again. No one was certain how the Alien Beings spotted the convoy, but they believed the initial sighting was by Alien Beings in the fields the convoy had passed. The subsequent targeting may have been the work of sensors on the asteroid ship itself.

****

General Hawk pulled into Leechburg more than forty-five hours after leaving Colorado. There was no fanfare. Rooms had been set up in various houses spread out around the communities. The general and his staff stayed at what had been a bed and breakfast inside an old church in downtown Leechburg. As leadership members arrived, crews dispersed the leaders' vehicles throughout the outlying communities so they would not draw any attention.

A contingent of several cars was pre-positioned under the Leechburg bridge and camouflaged, ready for a quick getaway, if needed. Chip and other key personnel were purposely left out of the meetings, just in case the meetings' participants fell victim to the Alien Being particle beam, or some other unknown calamity. Without exception, the nuclear submarine was ordered to fire nuclear weapons at all three Alien Being locations, and Chip was to assume the presidency if no other word came in the next two weeks.

****

Heading north on I-29 toward Sioux City, Iowa, for its destination of Wright Patterson AFB, a routine courier team from Offutt started its run across the wastelands. The courier team was just out of limits of the former city of Omaha, and into Council Bluffs, Iowa, when the entire area to the south of them erupted in a tremendous explosion, much larger than anything experienced by the radio teams or other couriers. A mushroom cloud formed, extending miles into the sky over the former Offutt Air Force Base. The ground shook and subsequent concussions popped their ears.

"Oh my God!" was all one courier could say to the other as he looked back at the mushroom cloud that was once Offutt AFB and his home for the last two years.

Well over a hundred lives were snuffed out in an instant.

The other courier was caught somewhere between fear and anger, watching the cloud rise. After seeing the explosion in their rear view mirror of the Omaha and the base, couriers drove non-stop to Wright Patterson as fast as they as they could with safety. At Wright Patterson, another courier team drove to Leechburg along with a member of the Nebraska team to inform the leadership conference about the destruction of Offutt AFB.

Upon hearing the news, the officer in charge at Wright Patterson ordered the evacuation of all non-essential civilian personnel, and a subset of the scientists. They were to wait at a location in the countryside until they received word to return.

CHAPTER 39
The Plan

"Simplicity is the ultimate sophistication."
LEONARDO DA VINCI

The president gathered his military leaders together for a strategy summit in Leechburg. The participants would use the Colonel's cave compound as a meeting place.

The president opened the summit by saying, "The earth has been invaded by aliens. They first sent pods to plant seeds, then subsequently sent landing ships."

Everyone already knew this but it hit all like a ton of bricks to have the president saying it to them in person.

The president went on to say, "The asteroid strikes appear deliberate and directly related to the Alien Beings' arrival. In the real world, aliens are not going to come down like the movie *Independence Day*, wait many hours, and then attack with ray guns; if you were an alien civilization, you'd drop asteroids on a planet to first clear it of its indigenous life, if not wanted. Time is on your side when traveling through the vastness of space in suspended animation."

President Stockwell then related his plan to destroy the Russian and African Alien Being settlements outright with nuclear weapons from the United States' only known remaining nuclear submarine. Additionally, the battle plan called for damaging the asteroid particle beam and immobilizing but not entirely destroying the remaining Alien Being settlement in Iowa. The president said that he did not want any nukes used directly on US soil. Also, he said he believed it prudent to keep some of the Alien Beings alive as an incentive to their leaders not to drop more asteroids on the planet. If the intel obtained from the abducted Alien Beings was accurate, the last of their species would reside in the settlement in Iowa.

President Stockwell turned over the meeting to General Hawk to discuss the specific military aspects of the plan.

General Hawk started off by saying, "The plan is to immobilize the particle beam on the asteroid ship; however, we will need to identify the exact location of this weapon system." The general paused to let folks take in what he said. The other military leaders had the question on the tips of their tongue, but did not ask how they were to find the particle beam on a 100-mile-wide asteroid.

The general then spit out several sunflower seeds and said, "The plan is to draw the particle beam weapon's fire on a target on earth and through triangulation discover the exact portal location using a spy satellite NORAD re-positioned near the asteroid. Another satellite, the NASA moon surveyor satellite, has already been circling the asteroid ship, mapping and cataloging its surface to within a six-inch accuracy."

General Hawk lightened the mood somewhat by adding, "We should make the young airman who had the epiphany to use the moon surveyor satellite a master sergeant for the idea, if we survive all this." The General reiterated in a confident voice, "When we achieve victory.

"When the exact location of the particle beam is identified, the air force will deploy its secret laser plane. For those of you who did not know, the U.S.A.F. laser plane, debuted in 2008, it is a 747 fitted with a chemical oxygen iodine laser designed to take out incoming missiles. The laser plane is housed in a bunker at a secret military base in Montana. Not Area 51—that was just a ruse for the conspiratorialists," the General half joked.

No one laughed at the General's remarks, and he proceeded with the briefing.

"At 40,000 feet, the laser plane will fire at the weapon portal on the asteroid ship. After the weapon is taken out, the laser plane will continue to take out other targets of opportunity on the surface of the asteroid ship based on imagery from the moon surveyor satellite. From the intelligence gathered from the captured Alien Beings, the asteroid ship is mainly a travel vessel and not a warship, and apparently is not battle hardened."

General Hawk then turned the briefing over to the senior civilian in charge of Wright Patterson AFB, Mr. George Vulcanburg.

"From experiments the scientists at Wright Patterson Air Force Base performed, it was determined that the Alien Being circuitry is susceptible to electromagnetic pulses, similar to the human technology vulnerability at the time of the Pacific impact," Mr. Vulcanburg told the group. "Older technology without integrated circuits, or with vacuum tubes, held up well to EMP bursts from the impacts, and that is why all the older cars and trucks still start. Our scientists determined the exact wavelength that best affects Alien Being electronics; these specifications have been provided to the submarine team, to adjust the blast for optimal yield. Once the Alien Being electronics are disabled, the aliens on the ground will be knocked back to the Stone Age, so to speak; they will not be able to communicate amongst themselves unless they are within a few feet of each other."

This strategy used the concept taught by Colonel (Retired) John Warden in taking out the command and communications of the enemy.

The president had General Hawk detail the entire plan from beginning to end. The plan would kick off in two days, with two radio teams attempting to draw fire from the particle beam. Another team, at a somewhat safe distance, would calculate the telemetry data for the portal location on the asteroid ship through triangulation. Once the location was calculated, the telemetry data would be radioed out via a mix of random radio transmissions.

The U.S.A.F. laser plane would launch from its secret base in Montana as the worldwide attacks commenced. The hanger for the laser plane was literally inside a mountain. Two hours after takeoff, the nuclear submarine commanded by Captain Bagley would launch three of its nuclear missiles. The general explained that the crew in Montana was now working around the clock to get the laser plane's runway ready for takeoff.

The first missile was targeted for the Russian Alien Being settlement; this missile, a MIRV (multiple independently targetable reentry vehicle) could deploy half a dozen separate missiles in a single firing and destroy everything within a 200 square mile radius of the settlement. The second missile would do the same for the African Alien Being settlement, and a third missile would detonate high above Iowa in the upper atmosphere to disable the Alien Being electronics at the Iowa location. The submarine would then immediately dive and hide in a super-secret underwater Cold War submarine base incorporating an underwater cavern complex. Captain Glenn Bagley and crew would wait for its next set of orders via very low frequency radio.

At the same time the three missiles detonated, the laser plane would attempt to disable the particle beam weapon on the asteroid ship. After the EMP attack, a ground team would assault and capture the main landing craft in the Iowa settlement and take prisoner the Alien Being leadership. The assault team would be ordered to take out any Alien Beings that got in the way of the capture of the Alien Being leadership. The main interpreter from Wright Patterson would accompany the assault team and communicate the terms of surrender to the Alien Being leadership. The interpreter would also relate that there was a nuclear weapon loaded in a van parked outside the main alien landing craft that would destroy the settlement in the absence of an unconditional surrender or in the event of any funny business.

****

As if cued by a theater's stage manager, one of the couriers who witnessed the attack on Offutt Air Force Base arrived in Leechburg, with the two fresh drivers. The courier was immediately shown to the Colonel's cave where he related the story of what happened and what he and his partner had witnessed. The courier arrived only minutes before the leadership summit was about to end with the various teams heading their separate ways for the mission at hand. After hearing the courier's update, all the president could say was, "We need to act, and act now! We do not have long until we are discovered and systematically destroyed," the president said. Gathering all the summit's participants at the mouth of the cave, the president raised his voice and cried out: "Let's roll!"

CHAPTER 40

Plan Execution

"In preparing for battle I have always found that plans are useless, but planning is indispensable."
Dwight D. Eisenhower

After sixteen hours of meetings, the leaders from the different military teams departed from the Colonel's cave. They began leaving the compound just after midnight, at thirty-minute intervals, in alternate directions. The plan would kick off by a radio team, a Virginia Military Institute non-com, Gunny Sergeant Frank Joyce, accompanied by another retired Army Special Forces sergeant who would visually confirm that submarine commander Bagley successfully got his crew under way in the waters near Baltimore, Maryland. The radio team was to immediately travel away from the Baltimore metropolitan area and out towards the Shenandoah Mountains to make the radio transmissions. Two hours after the submarine departed, however far from Baltimore they had gotten, the radio team would then transmit the message of the sub's departure, and this transmission would kick off the entire battle.

The first casualty of any battle is the plan itself. After watching the nuclear submarine get under way, the radio team departed the Baltimore area near Fort McHenry, as planned. The exodus from the waterfront was difficult with all the debris the NCOs had to maneuver around on the roadway. The two

NCOs were on the outskirts of Baltimore, just past the I-695 beltway on I-95, when the radio team's vehicle got three flat tires all at once from some debris on the highway. "*Shit,*" was all the old Gunny Sergeant could say, as the vehicle's tires deflated, making the old jeep too difficult to maneuver on the already cluttered highway.

The radio team had only had two spare tires on hand for the old fashioned jeep, and the radio set was too large to hand carry. More importantly, time was running out for them to cue the Iowa assault team and the laser plane heading out over the Atlantic. The mission was almost a suicide mission as it was, and now the radio team could not get away once they transmitted the message, not having enough spare tires or the time, even if they did, to fix the jeep.

The old Vietnam veteran, the Gunny, looked at his fellow Korean War veteran friend, a former airborne ranger, as they shook hands, then drank from a flask the marine had packed for the trip. The army ranger said, "This is it, bud; we are probably not going to make it out of this one; again, the flyboys of the air force get all the glory."

The old gunnery sergeant just took the mike, gave a shit-eating grin, and cried out, "Surprise Party is under way, I repeat, Surprise Party is under way, be advised our vehicle is disabled, we cannot move from our twenty—over."

The ranger smiled when he heard an acknowledgement from the midwestern team; he knew the mission would proceed, and their efforts would not be in vain.

The two old soldiers then kept radioing random military Jody calls over the radio, trying to get the particle beam on the asteroid ship to fire on them. They sang out, ""See the sergeant's face turn green, somebody pissed in his canteen—am I right or am I wrong."

The radioman in the Midwest radioed back, "You are right."

****

Fortuitously, the first Alien Being particle beam pulse came down ten miles away from the midwestern team as they drove away from their position at a very high rate of speed.

****

The tracking team began calculating telemetry for the pulse beam portal location on the asteroid ship. The telemetry team needed more inputs to smooth out the data so it could home in on the particle beam source, and the two radio teams knew it. Ten minutes after they started, a pulse beam hit in the middle branch of the Patapsco Bay, only a couple miles from the Baltimore radio team. Water and debris sprayed up over their vehicle. The old soldiers just kept singing their Jodies; both men had achieved a peace with their fate.

****

The old sarge grabbed his flask again and said, "A toast to humankind," as he and his fellow soldier took another swig. They each lit up a cigar.

****

A pulse beam came crashing down in the Midwest, this time much closer to the radio team. The men did not let up singing out their Jodies as they sped down the highway, randomly changing their direction of travel. All the folks at Site R, NORAD, the cave in Leechburg, and the staging area in Iowa could do was just listen to these brave men on the radio.

****

The pulse beam came down upon the disabled vehicle outside Baltimore. The two old soldiers never felt a thing when the particle beam hit them. Their radio transmission went dead in mid-Jody, and everyone listening knew the men were gone. The team in the Midwest just kept singing their raunchy Jodys. The next particle beam hit further away and the blast not as powerful; the radio team just kept transmitting, not worrying anymore about getting hit. With the continual pulses, the telemetry tracking team kept narrowing in on the particle beam location on the asteroid ship; it would be only a few minutes now till they could get a lock on the particle beam source.

****

Finally, the telemetry team calculated the coordinates of the asteroid particle beam. Surprisingly, as seen from previous reconnaissance photos, the particle beam location on the asteroid matched nicely to a parabolic dish on the asteroid ship itself.

The telemetry team quickly radioed out the coordinates to the U.S.A.F. airborne laser plane and high-tailed it out of the former Lowes parking lot in Brunswick, Ohio, where they had set up operations. The laser plane sped across the United States, its sonic booms announcing where it had just passed.

****

At the same time, in keeping with the plan, everyone who had a portable radio transmitter started making random transmissions. One of the transmissions was a confirmation by the U.S.A.F. laser plane that its crew had received the particle beam coordinates, intermixed with all the other transmission clutter.

Fifteen minutes later, the Lowes parking lot in Brunswick was obliterated by the Alien Being particle beam, though not with the same power as earlier attacks. Flying over the East Coast now at 44,000 feet, the laser plane made its final targeting calculations and readied its laser device for firing. The airborne laser crew went through their checklists in preparation for firing.

****

The submarine neared the surface just off the Norfolk, Virginia coast. Three nuclear missiles cleared the water, and rocket thrusters subsequently fired as designed, thrusting the missiles skyward. The sky lit up for hundreds of miles from the missiles' blast.

Two observers saw the three missile thrusters and trailing flumes of smoke disappear through the clouds. The observers confirmed the launch via radio, intermixed with all the other radio chatter, and then quickly vacated the area. As far as they could tell, the particle beam never came for them as they drove out of Virginia Beach.

****

In high earth orbit, twenty-one minutes after the sub launch, the Russia- and Africa-bound missiles deployed as designed. Minutes later, multiple mushroom clouds sprouted in both of the areas. Buck, transmitting from the International Space Station, confirmed (in the mix of all the other chatter) that those two attacks had been successful.

Cheers erupted at the command center of Site R.

President Stockwell reminded everyone, "We still have a long way to go before we are in the clear; it is way too premature to let your guard down. Let's keep focused on our tasks."

This quieted the cheers and got the team back to task. Secretly, though, President Stockwell was more pleased than any of them with the reports from Buck.

****

General Hawk's men, a lot of them VMI cadets, had assembled a hundred miles north of the Alien Being main settlement and the presumed leadership landing craft near Newton, Iowa. The group readied itself for an assault on the main settlement in

Ottumwa, Iowa. The general had over 800 men and women under his command for the assault. The contingent of soldiers used a fleet of pre-1960s cars and buses; the general's team employed just about anything that would move and that was not susceptible to EMP.

The plan hinged on two things: the EMP attack being successful and the laser plane disabling the asteroid ship particle beam. This was too many "ifs" for the general, but it was the only plan they had. The collection of vehicles looked more like something you would see at a Woodstock concert, than an assault team taking on a technologically superior alien race, General Hawk thought to himself.

Knowing this day would come, General Hawk had had his NORAD team systematically position their vehicles, plus weapons and ammo, in the tunnel near Newton many months in advance of this day. One of the vehicles in the convoy included a nuclear weapon as an insurance policy in case the assault efforts failed and a bargaining chip with the Alien Being leadership was required.

The general had all the radio transmitters sealed in the tunnel in a Faraday Cage to protect it from the effects of the EMP until after the attack over the United States was finished. Just before the EMP attack, General Hawk had all drivers disconnect the battery cables from their vehicles' batteries. The general's planners had spare solenoids and other electrical parts in place and ready, just in case. With the tunnel a hub of activity, from outside it was not even possible to tell a single person had been in the area.

****

General Hawk selected Johnnie to be part of the initial assault team on the main landing craft. After bitter discussions with Missy, she relented. Johnnie could not argue too much. Missy was selected to be part of the medical team in Iowa to take care of the injured from the battle. General Hawk chose Johnnie as the initial assault leader because about half of the people on the team were from the area Johnnie helped administrate with the Colonel. The others in the initial assault team, including the VMI cadets, all trusted Johnnie unconditionally.

****

Without warning, the sky above Iowa lit up brighter that the sun, with the light expanding outwards for hundreds of miles in all directions in a series of tentacle-like fingers. You could have heard a pin drop right up until General Hawk yelled out, "Ladies and gentleman, it is go time!" His voice echoed through the tunnel.

The vehicle leaders reattached the batteries to their vehicles, and the vehicles started to come to life. Weapons in hand, the various teams then loaded into their assigned vehicles. The noise in the tunnel was deafening, the fumes absolutely noxious. The assault team was high on adrenaline and ready to go into action.

One by one, the vehicles drove out of the tunnel. Several of the cars would not start, and their troops reloaded on to the old-fashioned buses until there was standing room only. By the time the last vehicle exited the tunnel, the convoy stretched over forty miles. General Hawk, employing a combat strategy he had learned as a platoon leader in Vietnam, had the vehicles stretched out on purpose, to mitigate losses if the particle beam fired on them.

****

Johnnie was in the lead vehicle, speeding toward the Alien Being settlement. With him was a Navy Seal, an air force pararescue man, or PJ, as they liked to be called, a Green Beret who happened to be a Medal of Honor recipient from the Iraq War, and an Alien Being interpreter from Wright Patterson. Besides

Johnnie's vehicle, the initial assault team included a bus and several cars following closely behind Johnnie, guns aiming out of every window. General Hawk took a position somewhere in the center of the convoy to keep command and control of the entire formation.

****

The U.S.A.F. laser plane initiated the firing sequence and fired laser pulses at the Alien Being asteroid ship particle beam portal. It kept firing blast after blast at the asteroid ship—as many and as fast as it could recharge its cells. As later confirmed by a spy satellite, the laser pulses hit their mark, dislodging chunks of debris from the particle beam's parabolic dish; the debris from the successive laser plane strikes silently floated away from the asteroid ship into the vacuum of space.

At the same time, a spy recon satellite took photos of the affected area for damage assessment and downloaded them to NORAD for analysis. The laser plane kept firing relentlessly, only stopping its attack to regenerate energy and cool down the weapon system. The plane's pilot altered the course of the 747 to make it more difficult to hit with the Alien Being particle beam, but a counterattack on the plane never came.

****

A thunderous sound came down behind Johnnie. The asteroid ship's pulse beam blew apart several vehicles of the convoy. Johnnie had no way of knowing who was hit, or if it was the vehicle Missy was riding in as part of the medical contingent. He just stayed focused on his mission. With the fate of the human race still in the balance, this mission was bigger than any one person. However, Johnnie was still human, and he had to fight back the demons of doubt in his mind about Missy.

CHAPTER 41
The Battle

"Battle is the most magnificent competition in which a human being can indulge. It brings out all that is best; it removes all that is base. All men are afraid in battle. The coward is the one who lets his fear overcome his sense of duty. Duty is the essence of manhood."
GEORGE S. PATTON

The Iowa assault team's convoy reached the outlying Alien Being settlements near Oskaloosa, Iowa. As shown from the spy satellite photos previous to the EMP attack, the settlement had lights burning from within the dwellings and tents. The aliens' tents now had no lights working in them as Johnnie's team drove past them. The EMP burst must have worked, at least partially, Johnnie suspected.

As the assault team drove toward the main Alien Being landing craft, the assault teams only shot at Alien Beings that approached the convoy and not the retreating ones. Reports that the particle beam had stopped firing were radioed back and forth, though no one could confirm that it was truly disabled or had just stopped firing. This was all part of the fog of war. Johnnie was just glad it was not shooting at the assault convoy anymore.

Surprisingly, no Alien Being seemed truly aggressive toward the assault convoy the entire way to the main landing craft; the shooting of Alien Beings that did occur was most likely overkill.

As the assault team approached the main landing craft, however, it was a different story entirely. Though all the Alien Beings high-tech weapons were disabled from the EMP attack, the Alien Beings near the craft had improvised weapons, coming at the assault team members with what appeared to be knives and other sharpened instruments tied to sticks.

The fight into the Alien Being main settlement was almost one-sided, with the humans dominating; the convoy members lit up the Alien Beings with their M-16s and M-60s, and most of the team members fired out of the windows of their vehicles, cutting down the attacking Alien Beings in droves. The M203 grenade launchers took out clusters of Alien Beings now taking cover.

The initial assault team entered the main landing craft at the location it got from intelligence received from its Alien Being prisoners back at Wright Patterson AFB. While the assault teams entered the main landing craft, a smaller triangular craft landed on the roof of the larger alien craft.

The small craft was very similar in appearance to the drawing back in the Colonel's cave, Johnnie recollected as he watched it approach overhead.

****

The assault team cleared the large Alien Being craft room by room, making its way to the bridge. With the ceilings just under six feet high, it was difficult for some of the taller soldiers to traverse the alien craft. The Alien Beings on the craft were now getting lucky, injuring and killing several assault team members with their homemade knife weapons. The close quarters made it more difficult to fight the Alien Beings off them.

As they had done so many times at parades commemorating the Civil War battle of New Market, the Virginia Military Institute cadets affixed bayonets to their weapons and along with the other assault team members fought back the waves of Alien

Beings attempting to swarm the group. Most of the fighting was close in, and hand to hand. The humans were much stronger and more agile compared to the Alien Beings.

Johnnie could sense the telepathic communications some of the Alien Beings made to each other; they seemed to be somewhere between choosing fight or flight from the situation.

Johnnie "heard" the Alien Beings telepathic conversations between each other. Most of them seemed to be in shock, wondering why this was happening in the first place.

CHAPTER 42
Terms of Surrender

"I think that this is the first war in history that on the morrow the victors sued for peace and the vanquished called for unconditional surrender."

ABBA EBAN

Just as Johnnie and the assault team reached the bridge of the main landing craft, the hatch on the bridge's roof closed with a loud thump and there was a change in air pressure. Several much older-looking Alien Beings, scrambling up a ladder toward the hatch, were now trapped on the bridge with the closing of the hatch door. The older aliens appeared to have the same look a young child has when the music stops and he has no chair to sit on in the game of musical chairs, Johnnie thought.

The Wright Patterson interpreter communicated the thoughts of surrender to the Alien Beings. Knowing they were out of options, they reluctantly raised their arms into the air and surrendered. The Alien Being craft on the roof departed, its thrusters drowning out all other noise, even inside the landing vessel. Several of the security teams outside the main craft fired on the smaller alien craft, to no avail. It disappeared into the night sky.

They assumed from earlier intel that the older-looking Alien Beings were the leaders. The interpreter started asking, telepathically, each of the older Alien Beings to identify the top leader amongst the group of captured Alien Beings still left on the main landing craft. One Alien Being was deemed the evident senior leader. It was soon learned that the top leadership had already escaped, using the small craft on the roof.

The apparent senior leader was told to surrender all its fellow Alien Beings in the name of his/her species. Otherwise, every last remaining Alien Being on the planet would be hunted down and killed. The Alien Being was also told via telepathy that if anything happened to the humans once the surrender was formalized a large nuclear bomb would be detonated just outside the craft, destroying everything within a fifty-mile radius. The Alien Being leader telepathically said that its species would comply with the terms of surrender.

The interpreter sensed the Alien Being leader was passing the surrender communications to the adjacent Alien Beings and including the part about the nuclear weapon. The leader ordered its underlings to have the message passed on to all in the adjacent settlements, as quickly as possible, and that their species was not to show any aggression toward the humans.

General Hawk radioed Site R that his forces had captured the Alien Being main landing craft and several of the senior leaders. "However," the General said, "a smaller alien V-shaped craft carrying an unknown number of Alien Being leaders and what we believe is the senior leader, has escaped from atop the main Alien Being landing craft."

The General was unsure if his message had been received by Site R, NORAD, or Wright Patterson, with the main facilities still maintaining their strict radio silence for the time being. The communications were only one-way.

The Alien Being leader was told telepathically to have all Alien Beings, except for the other old ones, to leave the main landing craft immediately.

Other assault teams began completely clearing the alien landing craft while additional troops set up a security perimeter around the craft and the adjacent area, as more members of the assault team arrived on site.

****

The main landing craft was no sooner cleared of the Alien Beings when members from the Wright Patterson reverse engineering team entered the craft to salvage any of the alien technologies. It appeared that the EMP attack destroyed pretty much most of the micro-circuitry on the high-tech electronic items. The landing craft appeared to have only rudimentary emergency lighting still functioning.

Through the interpreter, it was learned the Alien Beings had no means to communicate with each other now, unless they were in the immediate vicinity of another Alien Being. This was due to the EMP attack taking out all mass communications equipment as well as frying the small receivers attached to each Alien Being's brain. The Alien Beings living in the communities around the main settlement were oblivious to the goings-on at the main settlement, except the sky had lit up and the power and communications were now out and all their electronics fried.

****

As combat operations started to wind down, an urgent thought hit Johnnie again. Is Missy alright? Did the alien pulse beam weapon take out Missy's vehicle? With most of the vehicles on site at the main landing craft, Johnnie did not see the ambulance bus Missy was assigned to as part of the menagerie of support vehicles.

Johnnie handed over command of the initial assault operations to Regimental Commander Van Price until General Hawk arrived on site so that he could find Missy. The newly arrived troops said about four or five vehicles had been hit by the Alien Being pulse beam back about fifty miles. Johnnie backtracked as quickly as he could, actually swerving around Alien Being refugees who were aimlessly walking on the road.

After about an hour of driving, Johnnie came upon the carnage from the pulse beam weapon. Bodies lay stretched out along the side of the road. Johnnie saw Missy's ambulance lying on its side, thoroughly banged up. He was just about to lose it when he saw a group of people with IVs in them under a large tent-like structure made out of a tarp. Johnnie ran inside the tent. He then heard a familiar voice yell at him for not wearing a mask. The voice then said, "Oh, Johnnie, you are alive!"

CHAPTER 43
War Crimes

"The first atrocity, the first war crime committed in any war of aggression by the aggressors, is against the truth."

MICHAEL PARENTI

It was determined almost all the Alien Beings alive in Iowa, except for the leadership, were in a suspended animation state when they left their home planet over 3,200 years ago. From the abductees' debriefings at Wright Patterson and subsequent interviews with the younger-looking Alien Beings in Iowa, they all were told by their leaders that they came upon earth already in the state it was in and that the earth had already been destroyed by a random asteroid.

The Wright Patterson liaison showed the abducted Alien Beings the two asteroids' orbital trajectories. This left little doubt that the asteroid strikes were anything but a deliberate attack on the human race; and this was apparent to even the most innocent Alien Being.

****

Shortly after the battle in Iowa, the president called for war crime tribunals. During these proceedings, it was determined that the Alien Beings who had been in a state of suspended animation had no part in what had happened to the earth, and thus could not be held culpable for the atrocities wrought upon the human race.

It was a different story for the Alien Being leadership.

From the interpreter, non-leadership Alien Beings said that their leaders would be held criminally liable, even under their own laws, for the atrocities they committed against the human race.

Later in the war tribunals, one of the senior leaders finally admitted that the Alien Being overseers had deliberately diverted the asteroids to collide with the earth. The Alien Being leaders described how their entire plan came to be formed. Even the Alien Beings witnessing the tribunal were sickened at the actions of their leaders.

President Stockwell assigned General Hawk as military governor of Iowa. General Hawk required all Alien Beings in all settlements in Iowa to register. As part of the identification process, each Alien Being was photographed and had its hands printed. Each Alien Being had to carry an identification card at all times when outside their domicile. Also, each Alien Being had to acknowledge that it understood what their leaders had done to the earth and the human race. The remaining settlements on earth in Iowa had approximately 700,000 Alien Beings left in them.

****

Since most of their vehicles and machinery were destroyed by the human EMP attack, the same aliens who had come to earth to settle it now received assistance from their human hosts. They required water purification, food, and farming equipment in the months following the battle in Iowa. The plants that were seeded by the pods were now maturing and producing some fruits and vegetables, but not enough to sustain the entire Alien Being population.

The Alien Beings had brought various farm animals, similar to chickens, ducks, goats, and cows from their home planet, in suspended animation, to reconstitute and produce as meat in time. Though the Alien Being animals looked odd by human standards, most of the alien livestock and poultry proved a useful meat source for both the Alien Beings and humans.

****

One of Buck's last reports from the International Space Station was that the Alien Being mother ship had left earth's orbit and disappeared into deep space. The NORAD team used the Hubble telescope to find the asteroid ship but were unable to find the elusive vessel in the vastness of space. The Alien Beings on the ground were extremely angry at those who had fled. The aliens on the asteroid ship were the ones with blood on their hands for destroying the earth and almost completely decimating the human race. The humans captured a few of the lower-level leaders during the assault on the landing ship, but the real kingpins had got away.

The president and General Hawk tried the culpable Alien Being leaders. Those convicted were incarcerated at the reconstituted Fort Leavenworth, along with various humans who had gone astray.

CHAPTER 44
Coexistence

"The only alternative to coexistence is co-destruction."
JAWAHARLAL NEHRU

As part of the terms of surrender, the Alien Beings were to limit their reproduction until the human race completed their worldwide census and the human population caught up with the number of Alien Beings. For the next fifty years, the Alien Being population had to remain at two-thirds or less the size of the human population. Land was set aside for the Alien Beings in Iowa, as a sort of reservation. Regimental Commander Van Price took over as the military governor, using his VMI cadets to administrate the province. The Alien Beings were impressed at the fair treatment Van Price and his corps of leaders showed to all under their charge.

****

The Alien Beings were allowed to integrate in small numbers into existing communities of humans. The humans in the area had to first make the case, and then the Alien Beings were voted in by the enclave. At the same time, the human survivors in the east started moving westward across the nation, staking claims on the new open lands. Bartering was the main means of conducting business, along with the use of pre-1965 silver coins. Gold was starting to be used more for currency as well. With no means to levy income taxes on citizens, the deeding of land, usually in the form of bartered services, was used to run the federal government as well as state and local governments.

****

Both the humans and Alien Beings worked together to rebuild the earth. Distrust remained to some degree between the species, and will probably never go away entirely. However, most of the Alien Beings were no more guilty of genocide of the earth's population than the average German was of the atrocities committed during World War II. National radio, then television, plus telephone services were reestablished across the nation in the years to follow.

****

In the next growing season, following the victory over the Alien Beings, the human inhabitants of earth had an abundance of food at the harvest. The birth rate exploded within the United States. It seemed that every female of childbearing age was either pregnant or had a young child. Kaitlin gave birth to another child. After Johnnie and Missy came back to Pennsylvania, Missy was pregnant again in short order. The having of large families was highly encouraged.

CHAPTER 45
The Future

"The best way to predict the future is to invent it."
Alan Kay

The United States held its first post-impact elections in 2016 and President Stockwell was easily re-elected, with Chip as his vice president. President Stockwell's secretary of state was General Hawk, and the secretary of defense was Colonel Robert Steele, my dad. I served as one of the President's aides. The reconstruction of the United States accelerated with each passing year. Power grids came back on line in the various towns and then interconnected between each other. As the remaining pre-impact gasoline stores deteriorated within three years of the impact, engineers worked to convert cars to use alcohol. A factory was set up to make electric cars in Greensburg, Pennsylvania, using reverse engineered Alien Being technology; their highly conductive materials and advanced battery technology, with super-fast recharge ability, made electric cars viable.

****

Admiral Bagley completed his survey of the earth's continents. Humans had survived in pockets worldwide. The Swiss were the most successful survivors and had a population of over 200,000 people post-impact and were now spreading out over

Europe. Other than Switzerland, most of Europe was destroyed by the firestorm from the European impact, with the low-lying areas destroyed from the tsunamis. A hardy few survived in coal mines, caves, and tunnels, however.

Admiral Bagley found that other smaller communities had survived on the other continents. Africa and South America had nominal survivors, with the flu epidemic throwing them a double whammy. Scientists at Antarctica's South Pole had survived the impacts; the asteroid strikes came during their summer, after a lot of supplies had arrived. Their standalone generators and hardened electronics equipment fared well against the EMP wave.

****

During the tribunals it was discovered that the Alien Being leaders also had tried to spread the same influenza from 400 years ago in the months prior to the impacts, affecting mainly third-world countries. Four hundred years earlier, when the Alien Beings found the planet, they inadvertently spread the same flu virus when surveying the continents. Back then, the Alien Beings spread the flu by accident, taking out large populations of Native Americans.

****

By 2027, a bill was introduced to allow Alien Beings to become naturalized United States citizens, with limited rights. Each Aliens Being had to learn the complete history of the United States and study world history, learn English, take a loyalty oath, and again acknowledge that their leaders had committed atrocities against their new planet.

Many communities were now integrated with Alien Beings. Having grown up beside Alien Beings all their lives, and gone to school with them, most children had perfected telepathy communications as easily as they learned English.

****

2027 was also the year I was able to walk again, thanks in part to the regenerative medical techniques the Alien Being technology had provided. I had served in various elected government posts through the years helping with reconstruction. I was as a Senator to Pennsylvania this year. Even with all the new advances in medicine, the Colonel died that year. A large ceremony was held with a flyby of post-impact aircraft over his house near Leechburg.

On 2015, Missy was given the title of medical doctor by President Stockwell and later became the United States' first post-impact surgeon general, serving in this post for more than ten years.

This year, 2027, Missy gave the confirmation speech for the first set of fully schooled post-impact doctors from the revived University of Pittsburgh School of Medicine. A few years before, the first post-impact doctor was turned out, the first set of newly minted post-impact lawyers passed their bar exam from the same school. The lawyers beat the doctors by two years—things were getting back to normal.

****

The year 2032 was the most amazing year of my life, not that my life had ever been dull to this point. I was sworn in as president of the United States; I wish the Colonel could have been here to see it. I have no doubt he was looking down from heaven and smiling.

The country's population is now over ten million, with just under seven million humans and three million Alien Beings. The earth now has an overall population of approximately twenty million.

I won the nomination in the primary under the Progressive party. The Traditionalist party lost since most human citizens did not hold the Alien Beings accountable for the errors of their former leaders. At this point, only one in 700 humans alive are from the pre-impact era.

This was also the year I also became a grandfather two times over with my five other children getting ready to graduate high school.

****

As I finish my journal to this point, I am going on to a new chapter of my life. My aides and I—one of the aides being an Alien Being—are working policies and strategies to rebuild the country and the world. We also keep a watchful eye over the skies, just in case the rogue Alien Being element returns to strike the earth again, as it did more than twenty years ago.

****

When we're not at the newly built White House in Washington, Kaitlin and I come back to our home in Leechburg. I now live in the same house where my father, grandfather, and many generations before them lived, on the land my ancestors had earned for the sacrifices they made at the birth of this nation and repaid again with every successive generation.

We are rebuilding the nation again in this new world. The land has recovered significantly since the day of the impacts. Trees, plants, and animals abound now, both indigenous and of the Alien Being variety. The shells of old buildings are a reminder that all is not back to normal—not yet. Almost every time I am home in Leechburg, I walk down to the cave. I am still amazed at the Indian drawings. I owe my life to my Pap's good planning and foresight.